"Set d Phillyw... novel about a University City drifter trying to not only survive, but also
    stay connected to the twin wonders that are great literature and music.
    Raw and robust, featuring strong characterization and a dash of
    Philadelphia's rich multicultural history, Phillywood is an absorbing tour
    through the back streets of America's great cities, in search of a legacy
    that transcends the drab reality of every-day life. Highly recommended."

— THE MIDWEST BOOK REWIEW

"An interesting take on the cities we love and the transformation of 'Corporate
    America' that many of us hate."

— THE FEATHERED QUILL BOOK REVIEW

PHILLYWOOD

....

SCOTT MARTIN

....

DAYLIGHT BOOKS
NEW YORK

Daylight Books
P.O. Box 1105
Fort George Station
New York, NY 10040

daylightboooks.net
smartin34@earthlink.net

Cover photo:
St. Mary's Church on the Penn campus

....

For my friend, George,
a man with
Philadelphia in his heart

....

....
ABOUT THE AUTHOR
....
S cott Martin was born in New York City
in 1952. He spent two years at Lafayette
School in Washington, D.C.
He did the rest of his early schooling at
Hastings-on-Hudson,
N.Y. Public Schools.
He studied poetry at Grove Street College
in Oakland, CA in 1971
and took other important courses at The
New School, York College,
and New York University.
....

BY
SCOTT MARTIN

CHAPTER ONE

When the willows of love set in it was still winter and the trees were bare and grey. As the first few days of March passed, leaves appeared and they were edged with tears. The willow feeling was a sign of spring. It was within this dismal winter scenery that the willows of love found their way into Hoagland's heart.

Cars passed intermittently by the window of his flat. She was whispering below. He had many thoughts inside his heart and his feet ached from too much walking. His hands were raw and his heart was scratched in a vast pile of poor health and displeasure.

He felt like a student of life and the pacing and tempo of his learning were timed oddly by his encounters with fate. He had to learn more, before life experience treated him to disappointment. Many things in the life of a pseudo-student were instinctive. He never seemed to be tuned into an occupation.

As he felt the willows of love, it was for a chance revival of his heart. His eyes watered, his head like a rubber band felt stretched in tension and challenge.

Igla was really there whispering from below the floorboards of his apartment, or so he thought. But, no matter, Igla was on Hoagland's wavelength, wherever she really was. She thought of Hoagland and it was this willow feeling which she created. Through the floorboards she talked. Her lips in his imagination touched the crevice of time. What he did not know was that she might have been a self appointed Cupid trying to help him away from his ignorance.

Like at horse shows, his actions depended on composure and style. He was living in Philadelphia, Pennsylvania. There was just such a horse show outside Philadelphia at Devon. Hoagland was a writer - a novelist – and he felt that this comparison between horse shows and horse races, and writers and editors, was a valid one. He felt that un-known judges were awarding or subtracting points for his change in behavior and his writing productivity.

CHAPTER TWO

A horse and carriage for visitors to the city waited and the horse seemed like it was crying in the grey dusk near the site of his recent love's new apartment.

Andrea lived in Society Hill. She had lived in West Philadelphia when they were going strong. Andrea was nobody's fool. She had graduated from the Bronx High School of Science.

That friendship finally dissolved in despair. He shed a few tears over the wholesale past. It was as if a curtain had been drawn between him and his former friends. He was in a world of horses he didn't understand, but he knew Igla did. Horse racing and horse breeding were very popular in Eastern Pennsylvania. It took an elderly woman in a downtown restaurant to acquaint him with the horse expression for love making.

"You mean mounting the mare?" she laughed sadly.

"Yes, that's it," he said.

"Mounting the mare?" he thought with wine on his tongue; he'd been saying something like, "humping the mount."

There were grassy meadows interspaced between shells and settlements in the world of the curtain. The curtain could be penetrated. The willows of love could come back. To explain the motion: A grasshopper hops to the next space in the field, as the nomad goes to the watering hole. A hobo combs the streets in search of cigarettes.

Hoag's mantra was meadows. He needed a mantra at the time for his desire was almost spent. A mantra was one of the few things he could think of to revive his hopes. The image of meadows seemed to massage his nerves.

Around the time of their break up, Hoagland gave Andrea a carved wooden rhinoceros that a friend of his family had given him for his birthday. In return Andrea had given Hoagland a glass rhinoceros she bought at one of the stores at the chic Newmarket shopping mall (made of restored bricks and right on the Delaware in Head

House Square).

In Hoagland's wandering he had developed a nose for politics, but mainly the grass roots kinds like housing issues where ideas were just beginning to be formed. It could be said that a political condition had arisen. There were many factions, views, people, and devices used to complicate the atmosphere of the University of Pennsylvania. Old friends and enemies congregated around the campus buildings. Arguments waged between attorneys, brokers, artists, government and University officials.

In Philadelphia there were two rivers. The Delaware ran curiously along the state border north and west of Philadelphia and ran from Philadelphia south into the Atlantic Ocean near Wilmington, Delaware. The second river was the Schuylkill, (pronounced Skoolkill.) The Schuylkill bisected the city of Philadelphia. The Delaware was used chiefly as a function of industry in the immediate Philadelphia area, serving barges, oil tankers, and ocean going vessels of other kinds.

Large freighters came through the Delaware Bay and north on the Delaware into Philadelphia where they docked.

The docks served an important part of Center City Philadelphia. In some cities the docks were miles away from the core of the city but this was not so in Philadelphia and a business person could leave his office for lunch and stroll along the riverfront viewing the newly arrived ships.

The Schuylkill was of ample width and curled at a southeasterly angle to Philadelphia, traveling thirty miles from Reading. It emptied into the Delaware in southwest Philadelphia. This was at a place many oil refineries were located. Tankers traveled short distances on the Schuylkill to terminals here. The Schuylkill was criss-crossed by bridges which carried traffic from West Philadelphia to Center City.

There were many street cars in Philadelphia and Hoagland on occasion had gone southwest and stood at the intersection of two or three subway surface car lines. Subway surface cars were like streetcars outside, yet they also ran part of their routes in tunnels.

The area in southwest Philly where two or three car lines merged was mostly residential with two and three story homes. Almost every house in residential Philly had a front porch. The west, north, and southwest had many low income areas, but within these depressed areas was the idea that a man could own his own home. Philly had a fifty-five percent black population.

CHAPTER THREE

That old feeling of love for love itself never ended in Hoagland. He couldn't leave Philadelphia without some resolution. Broadkey, Andrea, Douglas, Jerry, Mrs. Leum, "The Sad Man," Missy Tillison, Paco all came through the gates, acting like the pony Hoagland had simulated himself to be in this time of disturbance. No shots had been fired, no punches thrown, no rocks hurled, only the threat was in the air. It was a time of closeness replaced by distrust. A time of well kept secrets revealed. It was a time when emotional disturbance had to be thwarted. Like a pony, Hoagland had many false starts at thwarting his own flak. He counted himself out of his old crowd in New York where Hoagland hailed from. He thought and hoped that with each glass of wine the Philadelphians drank that there would be some progressive end. It was the City of Brotherly Love wasn't it???? An end where more people were free of poverty, an end where art flourished.

He tried to advocate peace in times of possible troubles, yet his hard edges didn't inspire peace. It had become a game of tactical maneuvers for him to reorganize himself so that he might one day find the peaceful meadow. Like a dog, he chased the bait of meadowly love which the whispering woman dangled before him and like a bull, he came undone as the imagery fluttered uncertainly through his half broken heart.

CHAPTER FOUR, MRS. LEUM

Mrs. Leum perched birdlike over her groceries. She swept the floor clean and poured a glassful of iced tea in her cup as she sat in the dark kitchen.

The apartment was a railroad flat and the groceries lay on the counter. The refrigerator was old and frayed heads of lettuce wilted in the compartment. Mrs. Leum, Hoagland imagined many things of. He thought he knew Mrs. Leum better than he did. Mrs. Leum lived in Yonkers, N.Y.

In the strata of the two mid-towns, New York and Philadelphia, were many sophisticated people, but Hoagland was stricken by abrasive thoughts in a tunnel of intellectual lovers. There had to be a turning point for his morale. Everyone had a sweet tooth for dance, love making, and rich food. The idea of riches was one he'd never given much thought to, but he'd been overwhelmed by their existence and a touch of desire further abraded his thinking. Restaurants sprouted in abundance in the crests of the two cities and the people who profited buttered their steaks and clinked their glasses in travelers' sunsets as law officers looked on wondering of the approaching decadence. It wasn't that decadence was new, it was new for Hoagland to realize the causes of decadence.

The drug scene had been labeled decadent by the conservatives, and the mayor kept West Philly free of street dealers that year. Some of the business people liked to see themselves on the angelic side of decadence but the word could have applied to decaying architecture and dying people in hospitals.

Hoagland had worked two jobs in Philly, first at Philadelphia Yellow Cab and then at Burns Security. He listed his occupation as novelist at the time of these events and wished he could have made better inroads establishing dialogues. In Philadelphia, the publishing world he became aware of was, The Philadelphia Inquirer, The Philadelphia Bulletin (now passed away), The Philadelphia Daily News, The South Bank Times, The

Saturday Evening Post, J.B. Lippincott, Chilton, (a C.B.S. subsidiary), W.B. Saunders, an education textbook press, and of course, Franklin Books.

In New York there was The New York Times, The New York Post, The New York Daily News, The Village Voice, hundreds of magazines, Putnam, Charles Scribner, Harper Collins and McGraw-Hill.

In Boston was The Boston Globe, The Boston Herald Traveler, The Boston Phoenix, Atlantic Monthly, Atlantic Little Brown and Houghton Mifflin.

Hoagland had the heart and a vision to be published but what was going on behind him wasn't clear.

Because Hoagland's old friends didn't call him he thought the worst of them like they were involved in a conspiracy bent on driving him crazy. He felt connected to the big time and advertising like one company wanted him straight but hoped the second company was still recalling Hoagland's stoned days to create scenes.

Some people in the health field seemed to be making a bid to manage Hoagland. The health field included hospital administration, physical health care and mental health. Since Hoagland was so young, many big ideas weren't completely understood and he became a prospect for the mental health program; he would lose his head walking around the campus and spit out his heart. That is, thoughts about Nina, Andrea, Candy and more talk about big time boxing hadn't yet faded from the press, how Muhammed Ali had bought a two million dollar horse farm in suburban Philadelphia.

It was in the pursuit of lingual formations that he tried to lose himself away from people. But he didn't know any languages but English. He was fascinated by languages and how they were written. He wished to find a new awakening away from his old habits and be rid of the dreadful patterns. He saw lust in words and imagined the flow of creative and sexual energies, but the devotees of the Middle Ages stayed ahead of him, or so he supposed and reshaped images to match their desire for quickly attained riches. He tried to forget, maybe there was more love involved than he suspected.

One way to forget when he got hungry was to imagine a river of grain for his gutted stomach. He could not deny the renewed pleasure in his pallid being when the illusion of Igla seeped through the cracks in the floorboards.

CHAPTER FIVE

Oh friendly faces told me of a lonesome way rainbows in the mist and early morning by way of a tree we drove through the pass of the river valley.

THE LOSS

"Dam's down the road about ten miles," the man said. He was a good strong man. A beautiful man, slightly bearded. He chuckled a bit as if he knew Hoagland's story, but strangely Hoagland felt calmed by the orange streaked sunlight. It wasn't strange that a rural sunrise would calm him, but strange that he would be calmed after what had happened. He had just organized his work and it all got away from him in the empty darkness. He had been provoked and incensed by his impression of laughing people around the campus, and so he had prepared his manuscripts, photographs, and packed them carefully, deciding to journey to Washington. He wanted to go to the Library of Congress to try and find if some of his work had been registered there by someone else. But he didn't plan his exodus from Philadelphia to Washington well at all and left at the previous sunset without a cent, using his hitchhiker's thumb as a ticket.

The barren terrain of the expressway entrance heading south to Baltimore was almost enough of a damper to turn around, but his Neanderthal mind pressed on. He lost his, to him, 'treasured' suitcase to an unknown man on the highway. Hoagland treasured his belongings for he had been able to cut an exciting book in Philadelphia during the bicentennial year. He had written down the name of a publishing outfit in Washington and had two schools of thought about his journey. He wanted to locate a record of some of the things he had written in the library and he wanted to talk to the small outfit near Rock Creek Park and see if they were interested in publishing him. The way he felt, his resolution about Philadelphia might come in the form of meeting somebody new in another city. He had ridden with truck drivers into the evening and became talkative with the drivers about his plans and the contents of the suitcases.

He got a ride from a man in a sedan who was just as talkative. The man took him to a rest area on the Delaware/Maryland line, (Elkton, Maryland), saying that he had to use the bathroom before they sat down to a snack. Hoagland waited for him in the lobby but the man never returned from the bathroom and Hoagland was alone in the coffee shop incensed. He ran through the parking lot, but the man and the car had vanished. Hoagland called the State Police and informed them of the missing suitcases, and then headed for the entrance to the Interstate. Hoagland hadn't been on an entrance ramp in a few years, and it wasn't a sentimental return to hitch-hiking.   He never even reached Baltimore with the luggage. After the loss, he elected to follow through with his instinct and head on to Baltimore and Washington, even without the cases.

He rode over the lights of Baltimore and into a suddenly unofficial looking Washington, penniless, at the time of night when the men of the bus station become frightened by each other. His stay in Washington was short. He walked around and a main street had been blocked off because of a bombing incident. The Snafus.

Hoagland tried to negotiate a ride with the bus company, explaining that he would pay them when he got back to Philadelphia, but credit was against their policy and he left Washington the same way he entered-by thumb.

The ride he picked up northwest of Baltimore was the beginning of his new hope. So it was that Hoagland's frustration and anger were subsided by the river and rolling lands of the Susquehanna Valley. He was rejoicing in the tales of a man boating on the river.

CHAPTER SIX;
BEGINNING AFTER THE FIRST ONE

There were some people by Hoagland's apartment in West Philly he didn't place. "Were they from the Eastern World? (Hungary, Czechoslovokia, India, or Russia?) The world of neutral countries and peaceful mysticism had him thinking. His thoughts swung and he replaced eastern bliss with, "or maybe in confines of stolen currency and hapless depressions of Philadelphia absorptions." Things were very active in Philadelphia, but the city itself was confused.

"This town has turned circles in the bicentennial era," he said and returned to his apartment.

"What is gold?" he pondered aloud. The meditations of gold were of high intelligence and in his poetic understanding, gold was a substance used for decoration. In the world he noticed, gold was carried around and exchanged for currency.

"Maybe the currency isn't stolen," he thought. He tried to concentrate on the meaning of gold beyond gluttony, but on the radio he heard an endorsement or a quick news flash discussing the Franklin D. Roosevelt Lumber Yards that were supposed to be burning. Hoagland didn't understand the announcement thinking there were no such yards in Philadelphia. The copy sounded fanatic, as to advertise the burning of something, someone. He changed the dial and a religious orator spoke of an upcoming hell so terrible as to want to give up the fight. Hoagland didn't understand that the preacher was trying to exhalt his audience to overcome the obstacles. Beyond all conditions was the price of solitude amongst the mongering wickedness that some street conditions create. There was wickedness to cure, eventually he would have to get the preachers' help.

As Hoagland had just begun to see how long some unseen eyes had associated him with decadence, he realized that those who dedicated themselves to decadence's end, hadn't tried to seek him. Hoagland was not yet a master magician and saw some dealers as evil who were providing energy for spiritual masters.

He found that intellectuals had whims to find an intellectual vacation. The higher education crowd in his age group had cut him adrift even though he still identified with them.

"Who are the intellectuals," asked a fellow in the Penn library who was trying to understand him.

"It's my parents, they have B.A.'s in liberal arts and talk about the collegiate scene. In a way they have signaled that I have failed them by trying the log cabin approach."

"Aren't you learning something from being here?" asked the student.

"Yes, a lot. Penn's libraries are full of

inspiring books and information," said Hoagland. The Penn library was opened to the general public in 1976.

Hoagland needed some guidance. Not vocational guidance, but help in seeing the light in what he was already doing. But there was no guidance for him. It was all in the books for him to find.

A few of the regulars on the campus who had spotted him in the cafeteria and in the pub were happy to see Hoagland disheartened and tortured in a blaze of hell, but there were a few sober souls who frequented the river pubs who advised Hoagland when he clenched his fists in frustration.

"Don't play their game."

He heard advice like that as he struggled to solve his problems. A few other not so sober fellows lifted his spirits one evening in a bar by shouting, "Let's stay with the kid." Hoagland was twenty at the time and they were referring to Hoagland's tug-of-war with Philadelphia's publishing establishment.

There were, as aforementioned, intelligent

people who knew the pivotal things which caused harmony and disharmony. There is a difference between an intelligence agent and an intelligence expert. An expert studied various countries and was an employee of his or her particular government, trying to gain knowledge in a given field. There were many such people around the Old University of Pennsylvania in the days of Phillywood. An agent moved at a faster pace and knew why stories of shootings and espionage made the papers.

Hoagland had had some experience with a rock and roll agent who moved very fast. Hoagland might have been over impressed by him, for doing things too quickly was usually what threw him off.

This was the way the whole mess started. He'd gone desperately to New York with his suitcases the year before needing to sell their contents and made phone calls to disinterested companies, distributing haphazardly his carefully conceived work.

As he sobered from the resentment the

veterans felt for his curiosity, he looked to reading in general to increase his depth of understanding, but at that moment his thoughts were very diffused and fragmented and concentrating on finishing any one book was difficult.

Hoagland had two favorite bars in West Philly, Le Marin and the Vol-Tear. He had made some friends after moving out of Andrea's in April of 1976. He moved to Baltimore Avenue and rented a room from two grad students in the architecture school and then got his own studio at 40th and Spruce right before being hired at Burns Security on the Drexel campus. It was during that fall and early winter that he hung out with Broadkey and his friends in Le Marin and the Vol-Tear.

Dana Broadkey was noticably unsympathetic when Hoagland told him how he had lost the suitcases hitching to Washington and Hoagland realized he couldn't go back to Le Marin and expect people to buy him drinks and cigarettes and that's when he heard the illusion of Igla whispering to him, his despair and hatred were rejected in cold type of blue love in the night time. The awful feeling could surely be answered, not by police sirens, phones, or agents.

With the constituency of the campus community being very cosmopolitan, Hoagland wondered much later if there were even more international students than usual at Penn during 1976-1977. He was destined to meet a tutor who taught Hoagland some Italian. The tutor was from Switzerland. Igla had been to Switzerland a few times.

The veteran pro students who traveled from graduate school to graduate school weren't very familliar with some of the characters in view like the 100 year old black man named Brooklyn whom Hoagland had met near Temple University in December of 1975. Hoagland agreed to give Mr. Brooklyn a ride to the center of town to pay his gas bill and Brooklyn told Hoagland that mayor Frank Rizzo had personally presented him with a golden liberty bell for his 100th birthday. Brooklyn was born in Providence, Rhode Island and had once been a vaudeville dancer.

A few of the veteran taxi drivers had links with the schools. Hoagland saw himself to have shallow views of both the student and working class worlds. He only had six J.C. credits from Grove Street in Oakland, California and hadn't sustained any great work effort since leaving high school, although driving the ice cream truck in L.A. was good for the experience.

His thoughts returned to the illusion of Igla. The whispering voice changed through the floor and was playing more than one part.

"Can these be three voices? Or are they only her in the actions of innocence?"

Igla gnawed at him. When she felt the reasoning was leveled from his whispered responses, she halted her warnings. She wanted to free him of his mistakes. When he heard sweetness, he thought, "Are these singing voices not to be trusted, are they of an unlearned variation?"

"What do you mean unlearned variation?" asked the fellow in the library. "Maybe she had knowledge of some other sounds I couldn't understand, like the ancient Swiss language."

"A code?" asked the fellow.

"No, a feeling, a talk, a sense," said Hoagland.

A man had Hoagland's apartment under constant watch. He walked a German shepherd around the sidewalk.

CHAPTER SEVEN: RETURN TO THE LOSS

Hoagland was happy for the moonlight on the Washington Beltway and wished for health and happiness along the trail. Along the side of the road, were many obstacles and pitfalls preventing him from getting away from hell and into early peace.

There were shills on the street in Philadelphia who might have been from gambling joints. Hoagland used the expression, 'shill,' but realized a man is a man not a shill. Long ago in England there must have been an enterprising sort who wanted to accumulate great amounts of shillings and thereby coined the expression shill for his cronies in gambling ventures. A shill is a person who is supposed to be a decoy or cheater in a game of chance.

The older men on the streets of Philadelphia may have come from gambling clubs in the west, like Las Vegas, Lake Tahoe, and Reno, mostly this older crowd were spectators and backed themselves with hamburgers and race sheets. There was a negotiation in progress over certain gambling clubs which were being opened not so far from Philadelphia, in Atlantic City, New Jersey. The ownerships usually were the big hang up in a bottleneck, such as a territory which was to commence legal gambling.

The clubs were not slated to open for some time and the professionals tried to iron out the problems over drinks in some of the Philadelphia bars. The juxtaposition of the gambling referendum and the change of hands in national political control (the Democrats with Jimmy Carter had come back into power) was the stuff some historical wars had been made of. There were hints of trouble and uncomprehended influence in the winter airs of Philadelphia.

Trouble could arise in such a situation through mob people, but in a place like Penn, white collar schemes involving mathematicians, politicians, and scientists from varying countries were equally dangerous.

Hoagland tried to perceive the changes on the Philadelphia commercial scene. There was the Belgian waffle stand, the new Red Cross building, Grandma Minny's night club, and a new hotel in West Philly near Le Marin.

It was overcast by the campus. Hoagland was intrigued by the whispering Igla, who he thought was downstairs and he ought to have been intrigued by her because she was really a dynamic woman who could inspire all kinds of people. The illusion of Igla had been replaced by bangs and clangs and it was only up the street a few blocks where sweet music played through transparent curtains. The innocents in Philadelphia felt no threat of tyranny and lived in a garden unhampered by it. Hoagland felt weary. "How could a bar hold the key to a new wheel?" asked the student.

"I don't know but Le Marin seems to," said Hoagland.

He had been bequeathed in New York by John Barton with a plastic game which used dice and numbers. He thought it a subtle joke about the referendum for Atlantic City, but also a subtle hint. New York never took Philadelphia seriously, but the Big Apple had its headaches.

There were a few differing functions of exchange in Philadelphia. A new Eisenhower Foundation had risen, reminiscent of the foundations which made grants in New York. There was also a maverick association in West Philly which had replaced the 1st Pennsylvania Bank branch. Hoagland never found out what the uptown exchange did but it seemed interesting.

CHAPTER EIGHT: BROADKEY

Mr. Dana Broadkey was just waking as he came down the steps of his small hotel in West Philly, smoking a non-filtered cigarette. . Broadkey was a warm man; a thoughtful one and he expressed himself well. He possessed the wit to listen, the skill to act, and the ear to play piano. There were other imaginations in Hoagland's mind as he bumped into Broadkey who was carefully reading the evening paper. Broadkey and Hoagland had developed a rapport concerning publications and media. Hoagland was too free with Broadkey in their conversations, or maybe Broadkey hadn't been free enough to help Hoagland.

It was past time in the meadows of love and Igla seemed to be downstairs. Hoagland couldn't be sure why she was in West Philly. It seemed like it might be Monte Carlo.

There were odd characters who appeared in the creases of the dismal sidewalks. The leopard in the bell told all people about

the ponies in the meadows in search of sweet
love, tranquility and life supporting circum-
stances and told the old living in parks of torment and the pierced ears of other affairs in
Hoagland's mind

Hoagland had been talking to his doctor in
Center City about Andrea. Seeing his doctor
was a ritual. They met for an hour each week
and discussed Hoagland's problems. His doctor
was inclined to think that his affection for
Andrea was a lost cause, but Hoagland decided
to make a final try. He planned to buy her a
bracelet. The evening before he went to the
market and bought a coffee cake and some
orange juice. Here, he heard some voices. He
thought he heard college girls giggling because
they knew what Hoagland was going to do with
Andrea. He was gonna kiss her ass. He had
decided that type of sex was necessary.

Buying the bracelet wasn't an experience
he had had recently. For one, he hadn't had
a girlfriend for a very long time, and two, he
couldn't afford anything like it. But now
with the sweet romance of Andrea and his

security job, he had a lover and some extra money. It wasn't the most special bracelet in the world, but it was nice. It was as if he was going to a campus dance or asking a girl to become engaged to him. Andrea was three years older than Hoagland, she had been married once before. Her ex-husband lived in Richmond, Virginia. She had a long string of lovers after she left her husband and had finally settled on Paul, who she was living with in Buffalo when she met Hoagland. Paul was still on the scene in West Philly.

He wasn't going to a dance, but it might have stood up as a vague engagement present. She acted very sweetly when she received the bracelet in his small apartment. The thing Hogland didn't calculate correctly was that he still had a chance to get back together with Andrea. He had asked her to marry him when they were living together on 45th and Locust. Few couples had ever weaved such an artistic pattern as Hoagland and Andrea had during their six months on 45th Street. She still liked his writing. She was seeing other guys, but she was impressed with Hoagland's improvement.

What got him down was the way she whisked away from the corner where she dropped him off for work. Hoagland hadn't analyzed people who believed in adultery, but maybe he was still young enough not to be tied down. There was a tempest on the scene in the form of the women in Hoagland's mind. They seemed like goddesses who blew like snow, rain, and hail. All completely inaccessible. At times he wished to touch them. It was a fiery love welled up inside him. He was in the depths of lonliness and searching for the deepest truth. It must have been contained in the movements of mess in the depths of hell and devils. No, the deepest truth wasn't contained in hell and devils, it was contained in something placid.

He knew the Bible ordered discretion. Selling souls was distressing for all. Lovers and virtuous wise men of tombs and temples seemed at odds with each other over small matters of philosophy.

The foxes of the hunt tried to go to the wind reckoned with the valley of hoping and told sparrows waiting by the park benches to retreat. To step back into the darkness. For a wily fox being hunted was one thing. Hoagland was hunting for a fox and went overboard on sarcasm from time to time. Hoagland saw asylum in the form of a ragged New York bar where people counted their remaining fingernails. People aged quickly in New York bars.

It was time to recline and think for Hoagland. It was a while after the depths that a person thought of life and sun showers.

The radio talk show went on and on in his heartrending retreat, as the darkness grew and his depression flourished like fungus.

"Where does the working man really stand?" he heard a man shout into the radio. And yes, a few death matters had passed, but no bullets had been fired. A few weeks later, when Hoagland was suffering through his terrible loss of the suitcases, a pawn shop man had a twenty-two cocked at Hoagland's head, "Want me to shoot?"

"No," said Hoagland. Hoagland went back to the store after walking down the street a few paces like he had changed his mind, but the pawn man waved him away, "I was just kidding."

It was five-thirty in the morning. Two people sat outside the apartment talking quietly. A car made a quick screeching sound as it turned a corner and subsided smoothly to a different pace.

Hoagland's thoughts about women were some of the things he might have refrained from telling Broadkey. But on the other hand, wasn't a free wheeling relationship better to have with another man? Broadkey? Where was Broadkey? No one knew.

Hoagland was confused by Mrs. Leum and John Barton up in Yonkers. Mrs. Leum was his given mother, and Broadkey hinted once at knowing that Mrs. Leum had another identity but didn't explain it. John Barton was still in his early thirties, but might have been coached to know more about Mrs.

Leum. Hoagland didn't know, but he had to keep working and hoping for an occasion. Breaks could be made, but Hoagland was wary of the stock exchanges. He'd never had any money to make transactions on the exchange. He read the microwaves of the Wall Street Journal and noticed some details of different stocks. He was also enthralled by the Philadelphia Stock Exchange, which was a pretty big organization led by the Provident National Bank.

"Who?" he wondered, looking for Broadkey on the cold street in the middle of the next evening. "Who is making the off color radio spots like the one about the FDR Lumber Yards?" Creative news, as Hoagland called it, suddenly seemed to be Philly's biggest art form.

It was an odd pattern. He would have made more humor of the ludicrous spots and vanishing Andrea except for the thoughts of the newspaper death (shooting of David Knight) which probably was creative news but still there was some swarthy fellow to remind him of death's presence.

Sluggo contractors appeared in the doorway. The guy who was supposed to be tough, looked stoned most of the time, but Hoagland sensed someone paid this unknown man just to keep an eye on Hoagland lest he err too many syllables on the phony news or speak on other shady topics.

The man with the dog, emanating from the cleaners, looked sinister in the morning leaning on the fire hydrant. He walked his shepherd by the hoagie shop underneath Hoagland's apartment. The sun came out brightly, but he was lying face down in a dark room, gone in a swift river of holiness. There were pieces of carbon running through his bloodstream more vast than ancient wars, as endless as time in the debts of mercantilistic values.

"How did the cross currents effect people on the other side of the iron curtain?" he wondered. There were curtains and the end of the cold war had been created in other places before, like listening to Benny Goodman's

"Live in Moscow" album. Hoagland had never been involved in a caper with the East before and he shook face down, groping for holiness. Twelve short years later the U.S. and Russia became allies again.

As the administration changed hands, most of the critical defense contracts changed hands, including armaments. Hoagland saw well made advertisments in a black and yellow book which was a directory which auctioned such contracts. The new administration had to locate the new ownership and then decide on a policy. The changing of such contracts was always a tense time and it hadn't happened too often. Hoagland had a horrible feeling Broadkey had fantasized an evil end for the contracts and all at once he felt wary of his free dialogue with Broadkey. Hoagland was horrified by the hoods in the street listening to violent music, like Cliff Richard's, "Devil Woman."

Hoagland had been in the Lippincott Library reading some old news clippings of one of the Philadelphia daily newspapers during the time of World War II. He had some reason to believe that there were some people living in Philadelphia and Washington, D.C. who were helping the Nazis during World War II. He was trying to find a clue by reading the society pages from 1942.

After his study time, he generally met with Broadkey at the Vol-Tear and it seemed like the city exploded dangerously after their conversations.

One night, after some French onion soup, they went up to Dana's modest hotel room to view pictures of an old hotel in St. Augustine, Florida. Hoagland was moved by Broadkey as the older man bent over the book discussing a place he longed for.

CHAPTER NINE
AFTER THE LOSS

After losing his suitcase, Hoagland followed through to the granite buildings of Washington. Some of the government had returned from weekend retreats. Hoagland could not turn, nor retreat. He stopped with townsmen to talk. Even though Hoagland suffered from psychological problems the people would talk to him in return. The reason being that Hoagland was willing to start a conversation. Sometimes Hoagland had great cause to wonder why he was reaccepted by the coffee shop crowd, after the way he lost his head. He would sit in a chair drinking a beer talking in a steady stream of emotional short hand while the jukebox played. But sometimes he wondered why the rest of the people had nothing to say. Other people on the street were losing their heads too. The drifters on the corners never left; sometimes faces changed, but there was almost always somebody in the vicinity of 38th and Walnut. That was the way West Philly was. Some people came in riding taxis, carrying briefcases headed for the medical center or bound for an important meeting in a restaurant like Pagano's.

Some people lived in cheap, run-down

boarding houses and were losing their teeth and rolling cigarettes in the uncanny hamburger stands which removed the memory of The Chuck Wagon, a fast food place which had burned down.

There was an oasis of mournful islands in West Philadelphia and scenes passed quickly. If a person wasn't able to accept it, to turn to his rightful community, he was out in the midst of a pit. Hoagland had a taste of his idea of community on his tongue. The ideal of marriage as an institution was about his mind. He wasn't facing the possibility of a reunion with Andrea, so he didn't think of her when he thought of marriage. It was just a vague musing. He had been attracted to her attitude toward living and Hoagland had his own relationship with the passing scene, with the print-matter, but the people in his hopes hadn't been there so the social fabric of their relationship wasn't perfected.

"Maybe," he pondered later at the train station, "she had no desire to interknit me into her social fabric when she realized I didn't have one." Hoagland had had one once, but already still a very young man, he had been cast away by his old friends to pursue a solo odyssey.

The police seemed to be camping outside Hoagland's apartment. He couldn't figure out why they were there. It might have been for observation, or it might have been a regular stop on their beat, or it might have been for protection. Hoagland had found himself a resident of Philadelphia with some concern for events which had transpired in and around the area and had been warned not to be so curious about the ray gun killings in Bucks County. There were drifters at every corner, homes unfound, aunts moved south.

Un-numbered:
MUSING AT THE CORNER

A clinical worker reminds the guy who used to see a spotlight, of the pretty violets out by Swenksville. But the 'used to be a spotlight guy' isn't sure he's going to make it back to the music store on the strand.

The kid on the corner walks into the laundry. He's another student like the fellow in the library.

"I wish I wasn't here," he says.

"Wasn't here? You have a reason to be here. You're a student. Me, I'm nowhere on the outskirts of the campus," said Hoagland.

"I'd like to travel, take some time off."

"That's what I do, and I end up here alone. At least you know some people, don't you?" asked Hoagland.

"Know people? Not really, there've been a few parties, but not much of anything to speak of," said the student with a stutter.

At night there was dancing in the bar heading uptown. Hoagland entered the bar as a mortal after the hot flames with Andrea had waned. That was in mid-April 1976. The streets became sad without her smile. She had suggested right before she asked him to leave the 45th Street apartment, that he finish up his book and go into the bar more often.

By the time he had gotten into the neighborhood place he was on a downward trajectory. The man behind the bar recognized the change in Hoagland and watched with his interest mainly attended to his buddies, the regular customers.   Hoagland had been spinning like a top all winter and spring, the veritable book of knowledge. One could tell when he lived with Andrea that he was wringing with energy though he hadn't said much on his one beer visits to the tavern.

To the man behind the bar it was at once both a pleasure and a great sadness to see Hoagland fall apart.   People said seriously, "He'll never be the same." The sparkle in his eye left with her and it had always been the same story with Hoagland.   He had never earned a sustained income. to be able to stay with a girl for more than a few months. There were some evil thread spinners behind him who belittled his job searches and his ability to work that led to piracy, unemployment and mental health.

In the backroom some of the bright students kept the place more than alive. There was a scene in which a jug band singer had some class and offered Hoagland a hand, but the singer didn't understand Hoagland's problems. This was later in the summer when Hoagland gamely sized up the singer (he recognized him from some black and white posters around West Philly) and the singer tried as best he could to help. But there was something missing in Hoagland, his fires had been extinguished by the doctors' pills. There was no desire, no flare...his arm wasn't pointing in the motion he liked to have when he did things.

He had forgotten what he'd done in these days of tranquilizers and futile job searches. The papers lay fallow in his crusty room. It was the summer of '76—at first he was living on Baltimore Avenue attempting to drive the Yellow Cab despite the tranquilizers and found himself working the weekend of July 4th as the bicentennial celebrations went off in fine fashion and fireworks could be seen all over the city. He'd always remember being stopped by the parade at Ben Franklin

Parkway.

When he left the taxi, Andrea helped him get a room on Spruce Street where his writing lay fallow on his crusty table and it had died lifeless, though the content of his papers was filled with life.

The man at the bar was interested in the Philadelphia sporting scene and kept up (though he was an older gent) with rock music in the area. There was the Tower Theatre out in Upper Darby, the Bijou in Center City, Just Jazz, and Grendel's Lair on South Street. The sporting scene was of great importance. The workers sat back with the government check collectors and whoever else had enough money to get through a game with drinks. Whoever could get through was accepted. The Phillies games were broadcast on channel 24, a UHF station located in the Northeast.

There was a suffocating feeling about West Philly. If one didn't get out, the spanking, bright Philadelphia depicted in the local print world became dulled and yellow and the television pictures of the Phils in Cincinnati were surreal to someone stuck in the depths of depression. There were many people who never left West Philly and an equal amount who left the state daily.

So far this reflects the white crowd in West Philly, but one sober day at 46th Street Hoag remembered back to October of 1975 when he had first moved to Andrea's. She was working and he discovered the West Philly Speedboys home football field. West Philly High was playing South Philly High in City league play. All the players on both teams were black. The game was played in the mud and ended in a 0-0 tie. His doctor lived in Mount Airy and said he sent his son to a prep school, that the public schools in Philly were no good. And Hoagland noted that there was a complete group of catholic high schools in Philly too. But the clarity wasn't there in August at 46th and Spruce and would not improve until he moved to 40th and Spruce at the beginning of September and get the security job with Burns.

No joke, Hoagland was jittery and living on borrowed cigarettes.

QUESTION

Q. Did Broadkey represent someone?

A. Hoagland had never stopped to think of it much when he was on 40th Street, all he could feel before he lost his suitcase was pain over the loss of Andrea. Pain over the loss of his desire, due to the haldol pills.

He came off the haldols after August and the doc put him on some lighter stuff which got him talking and rocking a bit again when Broadkey introduced him to Douglas and they met up with Jerry.

At the beginning of fall, 1976, Hoagland signed up for a lit class at Temple University Center City campus near 15th and Walnut, where outside after class he met some mob people at McDonald's who knew the Delaware River clubs, like this was still a link to the mature Center City business and publishing establishment. Hoagland didn't feel that happy. He went into the Society Hill branch of the Provident with plans to make films and swing loans to make them. But he couldn't verbalize his plans and instead got mad. He would get an idea which made sense, but his irritation was so great he couldn't make two appointments downtown without blowing a fuse. He would walk out of the bank storming in the blustery November air with a few dollars for his next solitary beer, thinking of the worst place to have it. He walked by white flats of the well-to-do city dwellers and the swiming club, ranting to himself in frustration. He kicked and hawed. He was defeated, he was sad, and he was determined not to go back to New York or Westchester.

He did go home a few times during the hot summer of '76 and the suburbs of New York, had a curiously backwater look to them, like the boys had heard Hoagland was coming and had switched the party to New York, or to a lake in the northern counties. He looked quickly at the main street of Euphrates. No one understood, and a lot of familiar people had vanished as he had. Gossip traveled fast in the backwaters of New York, and in one of Hoagland's old haunts, they were most pleased to see that Hoagland had to suck down a few bourbons to find his soul, but those were the bar guys from Yonkers not the real Euphrates people. The bar guys remembered him from '74 and '75 as a lucky, but drunken cowboy with sores on his thighs. Hoagland didn't stay long in his visits to Euphrates or the Terrace City of Yonkers that summer.

The double horror was that Andrea had undermined him in Westchester as well as Philadelphia, having relatives in Dobbs Ferry which was directly north of Euphrates. The motion of the villages hadn't changed much since he was a young lad and he mused with a funny smile at a flea market in Dobbs Ferry one sunny afternoon. He was with his old friend Bob, who had gone to Marietta (Ohio) and Oneonta State. Bob never finished college, but he had been a chemistry major. So that with Bob, Hoagland was still depressed by the medication, and didn't articulate to Bob what being on disability in Philly was all about. He purchased a used shirt and a basketball to use back at the West Philly park where an integrated crowd played as he grimly returned to make his resolution.

But during that sunny summer of shadows, parks, and trees in Dobbs Ferry was a touch of Andrea. Her parents had moved from the University Heights section of the Bronx to Dobbs Ferry a few years back. Andrea had a degree from SUNY Buffalo in Fine Arts, primarily printmaking which is the craft of etching. She was well-versed in many phases of art and literature and her early days in the Bronx made her corny enough to be a big Yankees fan. Little things about the storefronts in the tri-villages suggested that Andrea might have been counseling with other artists in the area on her weekend trips from Philly.

Hoagland saw his own image change and change again over the period of time from '59 to '76, that he'd known the villages. It could be possible that he would always be able to pull into a gas station and bump into somebody he might want to know in the area and it was possible to think back to lover's lane and try and reconstruct love, but his thoughts weren't so scientific and the thoughts of the sweet laurel of the valley villages were draped in hedges and shafts of light in the morning. This was something he felt, and dreaded the fact that he could visualize too easily the sweetness that could be found in love around the chestnuts, maples, and greenleafs of the Hudson River Valley.

Yonkers was different from the villages and towns north along the Hudson River. The Hudson had it's own heart, it's own soul, and flowed on, no matter what happened to anyone along either bank. Sometimes it had been frozen, but when winter warmed and it wasn't freezing anymore, the river never noticed.

His life had passed, and like salt poured through the color of the texture of the Hudson Valley, like a Thomas Cole painting, time marched on. The natives of New York

City didn't always know a lot about the Hudson River Valley.

The timeless streets of his wanderings in past days were removed from the dulled pages which lay fallow in Philly. In villages there were sensory impressions caused by the nature they exhibited.

For Hoagland it was possible not to fall off his saddle into a pool of insanity if he just concentrated on himself and not on the thoughts of Andrea as the Buffalo flirter came out in her. She had lived in the Queen City for six years. She lived in a small apartment near Elmwood Avenue in the University part of town, part of that time with Paul. After she had graduated from SUNY she took a job with the Albright-Knox Art Gallery as a secretary. Andrea drove a spiffy yellow Toyota. Hoagland imagined she was in Dick's Cabin playing piano as candles burned low, and no man in his right mind wouldn't want a happy lady around. Dobbs Ferry was always Euphrates' main rival, so that seeing a heartsick Hoagland limp in with a train ticket to a candlelight he couldn't really afford was of no great sorrow to the cynical drinkers of Dobbs Ferry.

A village girl removed from him in ancient islands never visited who had lost all love in Euphrates after he had regained it with Andrea, passed him in the night. This was about January of '76. In the modern 20th Century he'd been sweeping the east coast terrain with Andrea in her yellow Toyota, on the Amtrak, and on the bus, like two hockey players. But she owned both pairs of skates, and without new skates the hundred mile rink from West Philadelphia to Westchester had changed. The rink was quite a spectacle. Throughout the skyways of Jersey and the industries of Jersey, too, there was no place like Edison with its wealth of train tracks, and the train stacion, and warehouses that lined the streets. Hoagland had been inspired after spending the night in Edison, like it was the turn of the century when they put direct current into the walls and entered the modern age of electricians led by Thomas Edison. His lab is in nearby Menlo Park.

Hoagland had started this thread with his father's knowledge of the book, "The Beer Can by The Highway" and then consumed more 'head' food about the megalopolis since he had gone with Andrea and they made their trips to Boston, New York, New Jersey, and Philly. But it was over, Hoagland and Andrea had broken up, the sweep's time was up. Hoagland looked at the old milde- wed storefronts of Euphrates. It was going to be a struggle.

MEMORY
Un-numbered
He was sliding down a hillside in Boston in the snow-covered ice of his wrong turn with- out his mind. He rode his wrong turn always looking to catch up, always hoping to pass. He had no special resentment for the Euphra- tesites then, they were orthodox, but maybe in Boston, four years before he had known

Andrea, his birth showed up in a realm away from the Hudson River Valley.

He was envying musical artists instead of really getting down to his own work. He got down to his own work as a singer, but it wasn't developing the way he wanted it to.

The Hudson's ways and beauty still held him, but he had been alongside other fire escapes, lawns and rivers before he had lived along the Hudson. He'd never lived in Boston and was there to find a friend who knew better than to greet him for he had written of Igla from detainment out west. Did Wentworth, his Boston friend, know Igla? Hoagland never heard of the pregnancy, but assumed it was a spiritual thing because Igla was a redhead.

He was in a rush of bullion far west where junks slept in the port and one heard the Spanish sound of the whispering tide underneath the bridges of another bay. Hoagland had made a big thing about comparing Boston with San Francisco, trying to study love as far as he could reach about all it's geometries.

Igla had grown up in Sudbury Center, home of Thoreau's Walden Pond, in Middlesex County about fifteen miles from Cambridge, and Hoagland had met her on Haight Street in September of 1972. She bubbled over with scientific and historical ideas during their three day friendship, but Hoagland had thought her to be two years younger than he. "When it turned out he was the younger, that was one reason that she may have decided not to marry him, assuming she did have his child.

His mind returned to Mrs. Leum and Euphrates and Yonkers. Mrs. Leum suffered from depressions which had to do with arranging her packing boxes filled with books. In the old house on Edgars Lane, roses grew up wooden lattices, but the railroad flat in Glenwood was hard for Mrs. Leum to accept.

Hoagland had accepted his change in status as people saw him currently as the drunken cowboy, lottery skater, lost a ticket, bum on the Bowery; they'd been in New York

City before and didn't care for the sweet scent of azalea in his memory. He remembered when his father and the garden contractor planted the azaleas and his friend Ducky talked about their "diamond gravel" which formed a patio. They were just white stones. "Let someone else win," he thought people were thinking.

I'll have to advise the reader that the story raced far afield at this time and one wonders what happened to Broadkey and the illusion of Igla outside the hoagie shop at S. 40th and Spruce kitty corner from the Penn campus. Drexel Institute of Technology and Philadelphia Pharmacy were also located in West Philly.

Three old guys seemed to be blocking Hoagland out. He'd taken his manuscript to J.B. Lippincott's Center City office in April of '76, almost a year before he lost the suitcases. The three men are his doctor, originally from Toronto, at Thomas Jefferson Hospital in Center City, a link to 1776. Hoagland also noticed a Thomas Jefferson Medical College in Center City. The second man is Broadkey, whom Hoagland suspected knew his doctor, and the third man is his father who he calls the "The Sad Man." His father lived in Manhattan and came down to Philly twice while Hoagland was there. The first time to visit Hoagland and Andrea and the second time to meet with Hoagland and his doctor at Jefferson Hospital. "The Sad Man" denied knowing Broadkey.

Hoagland asked his father why he'd been programmed out in Euphrates. "That's just the way it goes," "The Sad Man" had explained.

There were a lot of writers in Euphrates but there were other occupations, like the Department of Public Works, the Police Department, the real estate business, the banks, the stores, restaurants, and bars, and other kinds of business people commuting to the city, but there were some publishing types in town.

"The Sad Man" loved him and hated him, but there was this mystery about Mrs. Leum. Dana Broadkey was wearing a fine blazer in Le Marin one night when he mentioned a woman's name, Louette Jones. Hoagland's

mother's name was Louette and Hoagland
thought Broadkey meant his mother, that
Broadkey knew her from somewhere, that
she had more ties in the east then she pro-
fessed as she had plied Hoagland with stories
about her San Francisco grandmother and
Santa Barbara childhood when he was a boy.
Hoagland had never heard her mention that
the family had something to do with New
York or Long Island or Philadelphia before
she and the "The Sad Man" had been married
in Manhattan in 1947.

The United States was in an economic
decline, but quite a few people were still riding
Amtrak trains when Hoagland and Andrea
began making their treks between the two
cities. It was part of his self-appointed job to listen to the radio talk shows after returning from
his security post.

WITHOUT LOVE BUT, un-numbered

Hoagland was working in the menial position of a guard at Drexel University in University City. There were only two other white guards in the Drexel operation, a detail of fifty. One of the guards, a black guy from West Philly, kept kidding Hoagland.

"Hoagie, what happened to your green stamps?" Bobby was referring to the fact that Burns was paying Hoagland less than the minimum wage, though Hoagland had tried to appeal to the Captain.

There was something curious about the time clock a security man carried. It was round and hollow and hung by a strap from the shoulder. He used the clock in making the rounds, when he arrived at a key stop where a key was located on the floor in a dish. This key was placed into a slot on the clock and the key was turned. This made a tape for the Captain to check and see if the guard had made all his station stops.

Meeting Broadkey, getting another place to live and finding a job was something of a comeback after the crack-ups of April '76. Andrea had left Newmarket when she moved from South 45th Street to Society Hill. She got a little job off the books in a florist. She continued to go home to her parents in Dobbs Ferry without Hoagland during the summer and fall of '76.

Hoagland began to have some beers in the local bars. He hadn't missed the beer before Broadkey and it wasn't true that beer was why he met the gentleman, but that's what the bar scene was good for. Hoagland was lucky to know Dana and he detailed partial descriptions of what had happened in New York in April. Andrea was about to give Hoagland the heave ho, so Hoagland thought if he could sell a record or a book to produce some income she might stay with him.

The deck was fixed. "The Sad Man," Dana, the doctor, Louette, the publisher at J.B.Lippincott - all of these participants in Hogland's life had better all-round educations than he did. They had been in liberal arts classes writing papers on anthropology, sociology, zoology and concealed from Hoagland some of their wisdom in these

fields. But Hoagland's books and songs were
epic folk tales that were fun to read and listen to and were being sold somewhere.
When Hoagland brought "The Early
Voyages" in and two or three L.P.'s worth of
songs for the 1976 imprints, the owners
decided to force him into mental health rather
than offer him a contract, and that lasted for
twenty one years.

OLDER EUPHRATES, un-numbered

No one knew when walking across the
Warburton bridge, were the children supposed to sing to the DPW men waiting for
the sun to hit the Palisades in the plaza many
feet below and years before they had had a
professional wrestler in the old dust of the
ball field spitting.

Mrs. Leum's apartment in Glenwood,
Yonkers looked like a moving and storage
warehouse. She had 100 packing boxes
filled with books, marked Bowling Green,

New York, Connecticut, New Jersey.

Hoagland's brother John lived in South Yonkers. He was married and was a journalist with the Westchester/Rockland Newspapers. Hoagland noted that Broadkey said he had a brother in Chestnut Hill who was a corporate lawyer and a sister in Westport, Connecticut.

Mrs. Leum, as stated, was quite talented at not telling Hoagland what the older people were doing to effect his life. She also suffered from deep depressions. Andrea had written Hoagland a note saying she had met up with some young men with shag haircuts in Euphrates which was calculated to make Hoagland jealous, but he also wondered whether she had made some connection with Ducky and the old Yankees crowd from his teenage days in the Babe Ruth baseball league. Another problem was Hoagland's various speculations and jealousies that Andrea was having affairs with Hadley and "The Sad Man".

Of Euphrates and Mrs. Leum's boxes, it hadn't always been quite such a one way

street.   There were times when people had
picked him up out of the cinders, drunk; times
when he sat back and listened to fine music at
a friend's house, but after the mental health
number was called, none of his old friends
fought with him.

CHAPTER TEN: PRESERVED

Hoagland had diminished like a footprint
which disappears in high tide, after enjoying
a brief comeback on the front lawn of
Hadley's in Euphrates. In June of '75, then
again in April of '76 there was the red ball.

Hoagland had put on fifteen pounds driving the taxi in Queens when Hadley returned
from music school in June of '75. They were
a bit washed out and almost retarded playing
catch with the ball. "Ha-ha," like a cartoon
echoed in their faces.

In '76 on Hadley's front lawn Hoagland
who had been on a starvation budget while
writing about "The Early Voyages," which

was a log of what went on after leaving Euphrates High School, or at least accounts of some of the traveling with Daniel and Aaron. Hoagland was like a piece of leather and losing touch like a carbonated water gun had been flushed through his brain cells and he'd been with the tar pits track team. Except there was a chance for magic hanging for Hoagland on that lawn. Hadley offered to take Hoagland to New Paltz, but Hoagland was too desperately on the trail of Andrea and his creations were spinning around various offices in Philadelphia and New York. He felt obsessed by the loss of Andrea and hoped to gain Hadley as a piano player in the city. Hadley valued suburban connections and Hoagland hadn't considered the horror of hoagie shop living and might have profited by a discussion with Hadley in the woods by a waterfall, but no matter what happened, Hoagland was destined to be sad.

He couldn't refine or manufacture his gold for sale. He was neither smart enough, nor energetic enough, and he did not have the money to pay printers and pressmen.

There was the question of the cannabis that Milt had given him. Milt signaled to Hoagland not to call him, but the smoke set him off all wrong, like DMT; his hair flared and his timing, equilibrium and such were thrown off the ginger fulcrum they balanced upon.

He ended up at his brother's drinking bourbon alone where he made a deal with "The Sad Man" that he'd rather return to Philly than try to start over in New York. The New York record companies and publishers had all signaled that they weren't with Hoagland and Milt, the rock and roll agent he'd known from his childhood, (then Milt, had gone away to school) did not want to be contacted.

Some of this angered Hoagland. He wanted friends, he wanted fun, he still wanted Andrea, but part of the deal he was forced to make with "The Sad Man" was going to a mental health clinic. Hoagland was incensed by this, he thought he was being framed, but "The Sad Man" refused to give Hoagland even the 85 dollars a month he needed to rent the room on

Baltimore Avenue, if he didn't agree.

Hoagland's last testimonial to South Yonkers was appearing at audition night at The Eagle's Nest on South Broadway where he improvised, "On a Pine Street Production," the street Andrea had moved to in Center City. He met a big rock and roll star who invited him to come to a Greenwich Village club called Brave New World and play duets on harmonicas. Hoagland had choked on Hadley's offer to go to New Paltz and he fanned on the Greenwich Village club. But he did secure some money from "The Sad Man" to return to Philly, find a room, then he got the job at Philadelphia Yellow Cab on South Broad Street and ruefully began seeing the Center City doctor at Jeff.

The locals called Thomas Jefferson Medical Center, "Jeff." Here was an obvious link to the original '76 scene of 1776 which was what the bicentennial was all about, celebrating the nation's 200th birthday.

But stale air of half truths at a place which understood that a man's work was being used by the people who suggested he was sick was no cure and things did not get healthier for Hoagland as he tried to piece things together. The day after Hoagland took the book to Lippincott, "The Sad Man" and Andrea had said, "You must seek medical attention."

One day in May as she was leaving Baltimore Avenue after a short visit, she chidingly looked at him and said, "These aren't delusions." The sound of that shocked the numbed Hoagland's soul. He was under heavy medication at the time.

"Did she say these aren't delusions?" "The Sad Man's" having an affair with her. They've published my novel overseas?" "She puts her finger on my head and spins me like a top." "These aren't delusions she says." She drove away with the young girls scorning her in the paltry heat of Philadelphia and Andrea snorted, "Ah girls, but watch me dance my dance." Some of the girls did and Hoagland suffered as if he'd ordered a salt shaker for an infected appendix.

Mrs. Leum wasn't the pretty, sexual lady of her youth, but as a young one, she had morals, though she was a head spinner like Andrea. Andrea was a little bit wilder sexually than Mrs. Leum had been. Andrea could never conceive that the aging Mrs. Leum had inspired "The Sad Man" to become the glass person of marble ladies waiting in the dust of ruined centuries that she saw him to be and scoffed with "The Sad Man" at the depressed Mrs. Leum who was pitied by her contemporaries.

Hoagland hadn't thought deeply about it. He had had violent and intense arguments with 'The Sad Man'; he'd seen Mrs. Leum have even worse spats than his, and "The Sad Man" would wait as they screamed into the gale-force winds of futility. He would shake his head no until their eyes were dry and would, with a curt motion, instruct their next day to day move and then laugh for a second before he went on to other sad people who needed him to help solve their problems.

It was a hard thing to take, trying to forget Andrea had said in the sweat of early summer that, "these were not delusions."

AT THE JOB:

It had been raining for a few days at a time. There was a girl at his job that the older white guard had a wink for in his thoughts. Hoagland had seen her too, but no one really registered the fact of her friendliness. Hoagland and his friend were talking about Fairmount Park which touched both banks of the Schuylkill. The man talked about how it had been twenty years before, riding his motorcycle in the park with the ladies. He encouraged Hoagland to step out. "Don't take it from her," he said in a brusque blue collar way.

"Don't let any woman keep you on a string."

"Yeah, well, I gotta pay her back. I got to," he said, referring to the back rent she wasn't really pressing him for.

The man shook his head sadly. "Watch out for these guys, (meaning the other security guards of a higher rank) this is no place for a young man. You'll die here," said the man.

Hoagland found a promotional brochure called "Philadelphia In The Wintertime" left for him on the desk in the Drexel Library Science building. Or he thought it had been left for him. That was "The Sad Man's" occupation. He owned a public relations firm in Manhattan called the Bob T. Barton Company. Hoagland had learned many things due to his father's lifelong interest in civics, media, and commerce, but by the same token, "The Sad Man" had originally learned it from someone else too. Hoagland had already read a number of books for such a young guy and "The Sad Man" was always blocking him from learning more, maybe because Hoagland was ahead of other people his own age.

"The Sad Man's" major at Cal Berkeley was journalism, which featured a specialty in public relations. "The Sad Man" had never told him which advisor got him going on this. Then "The Sad Man" had joined the

Navy. "The Sad Man" was the editor of the Naval Reserve magazine for a short time and this might have helped get an account with the United States Travel Service later in his career. The USTS was a sub-agency of the United States Department of Commerce.

Hoagland had once put on a show as a young boy in a Pop Warner championship game between Westchester (N.Y.) and Montgomery (PA) in the Lower Perkiomen Valley, perhaps remembered by some of the Pennsylvania players and parents. "The Sad Man." had been commissioned for a week by the state of Pennsylvania in 1975 just before Hoagland had moved to Philadelphia to help the PA Bicentennial Commission plan their events. That delivering Hoagland and maybe Andrea too was discussed there, crossed Hoagland's mind later.

Andrea's mother was a little like "The Sad Man." She had been a health worker at a big hospital on Pelham Parkway in the Bronx for a number of years and supplied Andrea with pettifores and ampicillin. Andrea had done other things in art besides her abstracts which were similar to Chagall. She had slaved in a Buffalo print shop as a color separations artist for national Sunday magazine cartoons. Mrs. Lewis came to West Philly in February and took Andrea to the top of the West Philly Hilton for a drink to counsel her on her next move.

Hoagland didn't always follow Andrea. Their age difference, her being three years older was a factor. All her men were talented and she seemed capable of making them all happy, but it seemed that this frustrated Andrea.

Hoagland was still thinking about Andrea's statement that, "These are not delusions." He suspected she was in some way a party to J.B. Lippincott and "The Sad Man" to publish the novel written at South 45th Street. But Hoagland didn't realize "The Sad Man" was not his biological father until he returned to New York in March of '77. Thanks to his job, Hoagland was engaged in paying Andrea back rent he owed her. Worrying about the delusions meant that he was afraid he was paying her twice; once with the novel and once with the money he gave her.

"This sounds feeble," said Broadkey with an honestly upset face at the entangled mess of this petty trickery which had Hoagland so upset. But nothing else was to do so Broadkey kept listening to the sometimes boorish lad and found himself getting to the point of picking up his tempo, where he was in danger of stepping out of character and becoming equally as boorish. Hoagland wasn't to say whether or not this kind of thing had happened to Dana earlier in his life because Hoagland hadn't known him very long.

Hoagland shook his head sadly after handing Andrea the weekly money, but it didn't mean anything to him at the time. If she didn't want to do anything with him, it was worthless to have the money. She wasn't pressuring him at all. She suggested he send her five or ten dollars instead of the fifty he was giving her. He'd never given bills to anyone before, so he enjoyed bitching about walking through the windy weather to pay her. He was confused about the 'to do' surrounding the reason why she was avoiding her friend in the flower shop and walked aboard the launch-the Rusty Scupper Restaurant. In the bar, he talked with a fellow who had been a bartender in Boston. Hoagland could tell by looking in his face that he was an experienced bartender. It wasn't that easy to land a job in a place like the Scupper. The launch was permanently moored to the dock and took a picturesque look at the Delaware.

There were pretty women around who seemed mildly interested in stirring Hoagland out of his hockey and sleepy head over Andrea. But Hoagland walked away shyly, not having any real desire to do anything about it except look inanely at the Indian of the tobacconist's not thinking about historical queens like Pocahontas.

Later that day a fellow from the hayloft came into the Kyber Pass, where the lass behind the bar looked at Hoagland with a sort of joy when he came in. His habitual depression occasioned her to ask him to leave a few times. But this fellow from the hayloft was full of love and life and literature and was dressed up to be Ben Franklin. Hoagland didn't realize that this fellow's printing equipment was functioning and that it was possible to sip ale with this gentleman and work on modern material. A problem of old '76, this guy was white, but just who is Aretha Franklin, acknowledged queen of soul, daughter of the internationally renowned reverend C.L. Franklin, maybe they still run Franklin Books. Even though J.B. was all over Philly, the sign at 32nd and Walnut said that Penn was founded by Benjamin Franklin.

The woman in the next seat was returning from New York where she attended a fancy show at an art gallery and she was rather blase'. In Philly, the only way to be blase' with a cigarette holder and a silk gown was to travel in South Jersey through the thickets of pastures in between, some dotted with corn, raspberries, and sweet peas. There were funnily painted wooden signs and antiquated road trash from other times when people had traveled the thickets. Hoagland had wishes to meet people, but wasn't smart enough to realize the whole idea of Philadelphia was a theatrical show for people to produce things, and quartets came to play in sunny squares while playwrights did handstands on South Street.

Everything could have been fine for Hoagland in the sunny days of Philadelphia and it's festive mood even as he repented self destructively to the purse of Andrea. Of course he knew he had taken something out of the purse, so he was losing in his own mind and the minutes of the bicentennial ticked away.

He had been on South Street months before, when his hair was blown and the sea scape roughed against his face, like a lamp drying his complexion to the desired point of feature that he came walking from the yucca structure and settled into a small place where rhythmic songs were heard, and he talked with a man who was curious to know why people were being blasted by ray guns in Bucks County. This was something Hoagland didn't know anything about, but he kept it in mind. It was a pity, for his chance of losing Andrea might have been bad enough, but the way he lost her, under the large boards and gadgets of New York's Times Square district, brought back the conversation in the quiet Philly bar and he saw the hardware store in West Philly in the sunlight where he would go to make Andrea her keys, so that she might disperse them to her friends and him. He'd bought her the hooks for hanging her prints at the Penn exhibition, for she had signaled for the artists to commence in 1975 in November.   Hoagland was around the United Nations building in New York trying to help his tired brain keep up with his fast moving acquaintances.

Milt had some family in Rochester and could be a keen guy, but this day he was at home manicuring his nails when Hoagland limped in from a phone booth on the outside of the old granite station with the nude flying man and his testicles hanging off the crest of the Grand Central roof. He glared at the chrome wings, but later he decided it was essential in the restored designs of New York.

Hoagland was distraught coming out of the phone booth. He wanted to find a friendly ashtray in New York, possibly in the theatre district to make a transaction on one of his cassette tapes. He had a studio tape and two homemade tapes where he was playing the ukulele and singing. Funnily Milt had just the spirits to make a tape. Parts of Hoagland's homemade tapes were good, Milt might have had some thoughts on touching them up. At the time Milt was managing a group called Black Sheep. Milt grew up in Dobbs Ferry, but had gone away to Hotchkiss after tenth grade. He surfaced in the music business in Los Angeles as a desk man for Wally Heider studios and helped manage John Denver for awhile and even was an assistant road manager for Paul McCartney and Wings. He was thinking of starting his own company some time, but at this point he was working with older directors in advising Hoagland to concentrate more on the books, less on the music.

This was the cardinal sin with Andrea too.

She thought he'd gotten off the track with his music. "I thought you were a writer," she said, furious when he showed her song lyrics just before he took the train to New York.

Milt was an ace salesman who needed a push to get working. Hoagland didn't know him well enough, for he should have thought more closely about matching some of the plugs to transfer one tape to another, but after watching Milt grind his fingernails into an upholstered chair, no longer could he keep his mind straight.

Hoagland thought back to seeing Milt watch a very violent police story on television and looked carefully at the United Nations people with the neat circle of flags blowing in the spring breeze. He'd run out of gas, it was the end of his sweep.

Just the night before, he'd done something he'd never done before. He'd taken Mrs. Leum to see how he made the songs and tried to perform them. This was an audition night at a place called the Fair Harbor in Euphrates. Well, this involved a very proper

Spanish-American family his brother had gotten to know, and then Hoagland went with one of John's friend's younger sisters. They might have connected up with Dana Broadkey's picture of St. Augustine, their country was Argentina. Hoagland forgot the words to his own songs that night at the Harbor and his mother looked embarassed, but the coffee was good.

Hoagland forgot his mind after leaving the gentle quarters of Milt and blew confidently and wearily toward Broadway thinking he might have a final, saving way to stay with Andrea and continue his other work.

"Bad logic Hoagland! Go Back!" was lurking in his mind as he retraced his steps around the train station toward the theatre district. He was wavering from the weariness and weaving from the misting impressions and finally ground to a halt in front of a store with a suitcase. He rolled up his sleeves and had been quickly winded from the marijuana, (the stuff with DMT in it.) He thought, sweating, that he simply had to get to the

address of the record company his friend
Poe had suggested the night before and make
an impromptu presentation.

Possibly they would have the machine to
fix the tape up, he thought of adding some
music over his own tinny sound, still getting
an old fashion grain to it. He went back to
Milt's. Milt and he practically marked exactly what they could have done multi-track.

Milt had looked at one lyric and read it
before Hoagland screeched into the bathroom playing a rather horrifying echo on har-
monica near the shower. This undid the tired
Milt, but Milt suggested a player he knew of
and Hoagland got to his feet and hailed a
New York cab, talking in tongues about the
days of olden newness in a rather dangerous
speech pattern, for in New York it was easy
for a man to be sliced into the West River
when he talked in over-radiant tones.

"What is this nut with the tracks and numbers fumbling in his address book for?"
thought the driver.

"Here it is, let me see, up here, it's over

here, wait a minute, turn right, past there, what's that?" yelled Hoagland excitedly enjoying his ride over to the Theatre District, for lugging the bags did get disturbing after a time.

It was a madras day in New York, sometimes they had them when the panorama suited the environs of the wider skies to the west and splashes of fabric and texture, print and pattern, came from the carts in the Garment District. But he was north of Fashion Ave. in a glamorous section of the Theatre District. He hadn't memorized the whole Broadway grid, so this ride shed new light on show business. New York was a difficult hometown to have. A lot of people had it and being from it didn't mean a person knew his way around, for New York was so vast and intricate with many faces and meanings.

Hoagland lurched for the address and walked gruffly up the steps without a thought on his mind about what he was going to do when the elevator opened on a room filled with gold mementos of a record company besieged with hits and melodies. Airista's biggest star was Barry Manilow and they were watching a teenage Whitney Houston develop at the time. It was like a musical cake with a punch bowl to his eyes, but even in the confines of such a place, it wasn't good etiquette to explode into the olden newness sort of describing in a tin accent to the unknowing girl streaking in hose at the glossy papers enclosed.

Hoagland fell, exhausted; the lift which had lilted him cooled him down, draining him at just as quick a rate, so that the frayed edges of his rag tag demeanor and ragged shoes cut through the creases of his worn body and eyes. He was already thinking in a longer sequence and forgot about the plugs in his pocket, where if asked, doubtfully, but possibly, the fellows in and out of the offices might have helped him. But he was way beyond communication, and fell to a couch to show a poem to a man with an English accent from before the men in the old cos-tumes originally rid New York, Boston, and

Philadelphia of the English. Of course it was many years later and Hoagland always had wanted to meet a poet from across the seas and he was manically writing matching notes to the tapes. Hoagland tried to remember some of the tone, color, and advice he had learned in Philadelphia and Buffalo. It looked like a well-organized scrawl to him and he bloated up an incoherent, "Gotta catch a train," leaving the tapes behind, rushing for Penn Station.

Men on the train flickered, wearing checkered suits and vests muttering, "You've got a friend, G.P.I." referring to the Georgia Pacific Corporation. They were active on the Philadelphia Stock Exchange around the time of the Carter primaries and election. Hoagland looked at the newspaper dully, unable to see the print except to realize that the Buffalo Braves basketball team was no longer active in postseason play. Thoughts about the quick line of pot led him to think many disconnected thoughts which led him back to his conversation with the man in the rhythm and blues bar who was curious about the ray guns.

Hoagland was greeted unceremoniously in the large hall at Thirtieth Street Station. He'd ridden in more than once passing through the open air, past the art museum and the fountains, viewing North Philly where the buildings were red and ancient.

The hall was very active, cups could be heard popping in the cavernous building and men bought items and accesories as college girls sat with their skirts high on the leg, fingering ideas and thoughts of emptiness or thinking about their last orgasm with a boyfriend.

Hoagland scurried in and out of Philadelphia before the curtain could fall on him when John Barton came from Macon, Georgia where his wife's relatives lived. Hoagland had planned to take his brother down to the Italian market with Andrea for a real old Philadelphia get together. Andrea was tired of Hoagland and she ordered Hoagland to get out of the apartment when John and his wife arrived. Memories of visits to the Philips Mushroom Museum in

Kennett Square and the Longwood Gardens with Andrea when they had been snug now faded in the background.

Andrea's friends seemed excited about the tapes, but Andrea wasn't and he left with John Barton still smoked from the tint and staring hard into the image of someone across the water, which was another reason he should have been more sensitive to Andrea's needs. Ah, he'd done all right, but surviving became harder and he would have to go it alone.

The magic on Hadley's Westchester lawn wasn't magic. It was a feeling of altered reality in which things were not the same. It had been a carry over from the awful tumult involved with the tapes. Something fatal had happened and people were on the lawn the second time lying, but Hadley had no confidence in Hoagland, not in Hoagland's plan to return to the city. He assumed an 'if that's what you're going to do' attitude that Hoagland would be eaten up. Hadley was involved with stocks and bonds as well as his piano playing.

His father had died recently.

In Yonkers, there was a business street with Mom and Pop stores, as they were known as in New York.

Hoagland hadn't had time, or given himself the time, to think about stock options and continued numb and chided to Center City Philadelphia. He stayed at a reasonably priced hotel near 9th & Locust while he searched for a room in West Philly.

Hoagland thought back to the conversations about the ray guns in Bucks County when he should have been thinking about the tapes in New York.

CHAPTER ELEVEN

When he returned to Philly he watched the women in anguish and mourning and thought about the Bucks County subliminal light, like a frame per second of light, as in a strip of photographs aligned together. He saw the horrors of the ray guns and decided it was an eerie story manufactured by the newspapers. There was another death in the middle of town in the papers that had an effect on Philadelphia. People walked slower around Rittenhouse Square after the announcement of the David Knight murder.

Philly locals tried to play with his head as Hoagland returned to the corner in Center City to wait for the bus over the Schuylkill Bridge past the stone and ivy of Franklin Field.

That night Hoagland observed young professionals in society at Le Marin, the men were there to talk and the women wore colorful dresses, a variety of stockings, and tight shirts revealing the opening of their breasts. The women sometimes wore chains and lockets. These people understood the business school, journalism and criminology.

By mid-May of 1976, Hoagland had started living on Baltimore Avenue. He showed his doctor of psychiatry a song lyric that he had performed recently and the doctor frowned when he read it.

where the puppet makes a wave
to the con man he has saved
met with luck like Chaucer's wife
two of spades taught him right

It didn't matter much to Hoagland, as a poem he liked it, but he wished he could find less personal ones to show his milder friend, (the doctor), but the skin and the armour of the puppet he'd been used as and then realizing he had acted out in the role of, became serious tragi-comedy with no relief. People liked that sort of thing in Euphrates. It was kind of a suicidal place. They laughed it off, the tension rarely creased the area to the naked eye, although there was always pressure on those who understood the machinery of Euphrates. The mayor, the trustees, the police, and the volunteer fire departments. Hoagland's skin was chafed too acutely to make any conclusions.

He loved the "The Sad Man" and hated him. Over the years it was confusing and time for love was now Hoagland's hope. He thought about the president of the Board of Education in Euphrates. He and his family had been good people. Where had they gone? What was the future of the suburbs?

Igla sighed below the floorboards and old inhabitants of the United States forgot their wars, their losses, only to view more recent ruins, for they had to sail to get to the matter more often than before. Games continued in the mill towns of the inlands amongst some grumbling. As in Huntington, West Virginia and Ashland, Kentucky.

The liberals wanted to change the drug laws. Hoagland thought the law enforcement in the Hudson Valley had been liberal and fairly understanding of the positive benefits of a drug culture that the joys of magic could be shared with those not brave enough to try while drugs were illegal. Hoagland thought legalizing marijuana and maybe safe forms of a few other drugs would have to be approved by the Federal Drug Administration and regulated by a commission set up, like the Alcoholic Beverage Commission. The use of drugs then ideally would be taught at home, like a father giving his son his first finger of beer.

In Philadelphia, friends came, feeling for Philadelphia and it's battle. They found things more pleasing than they had expected, for in the old country, Philadelphia had a history of freedom, but an image of dubious merit. A brown haired man spoke in broken, thick syllables near an ice cream parlour, worrying about his camera and right exposure to the light. Philadelphia had expected many millions more than had arrived to come to see their city and the rebuilding and relocating of the Liberty Bell. Philadelphia had had many foreign visitors before, but this was special. It had been quite a long time since this many visitors had been expected, but Broadkey remembered a time in the early fifties when Philly was a travel center. Broadkey was the only man Hoagland knew who remembered the last era.

There were many others in more lush

meadows and some tucked away at the car intersections who understood and some of the younger people felt a resurgence occur in the present with memories of the old days of their infancy. And there was the motorcycle man in the park, where the old 1876 Centennial buildings stood and he kissed a girl, oblivious to make it golden, but knew of the golden women the old era had attracted.

The seaboard was always in motion, so the individual cities sometimes couldn't be separated and at the mouth of the Delaware was the Atlantic where freighters and tankers stopped in Wilmington. Hoagland had thought about Delaware and South Philly much earlier in his life as a drunken sot on the streets of San Francisco—a city sometimes mistaken for luv. The love didn't exactly drip from the streets as people who went there thought it might; it was however a beautiful setting for romance. One of Andrea's best friends, Kerry, was a graduate of the Penn business school and knew a lot about San Francisco.

Hoagland had tried to find love in a beer glass in the Haight so he stumbled upon a wayfarer from none other than Philadelphia. He'd never met anyone from Philly before and they really had some fun partying with cool hippies in the Haight. They exchanged cognac and nuts. This was back in '72, the man wore a McGovern for President button and said his name was "South Philly Joey."

Wilmington, Delaware was another place he'd seen from the highway in travels from Washington, D.C. to New York and Vermont as a child, but he had not explored Wilmington, finally witnessing only a wisp of it from the train window as the winter lamp sun of frosty clouds of breath came on.

He was near a relatively obscure area (Christiana, Delaware) when he lost the suitcases, but in Philadelphia, one of Andrea's friends was from Wilmington. Hoagland didn't know what to do about some of the things going on in his mind, but resist the echoes of former hatreds.

SPIRIT IN LOSSES

Mr. Readley, Milt's father, was quite a fellow. He set up in style in the Houston Hall building of the campus a poster board easel explaining the Jewish faith. Hoagland was touchy, he'd just returned through the calming outlands beyond Philadelphia, past hexed barns and pastures, the touristy stands, the residences, the colonial homes, the bricked apartments bordering City Line Avenue. On City Line, he got to Lancaster Avenue, walking in the sunny morn under old bridges through the heart of the old section of West Philly where the fish store was. A black man at his job had told him about the fish store. When he got to Houston Hall, he was touchy.

Vast twilight of the chambers judicial men opened from Hoagland's view of Washington. Just what did the judges and lawmakers do? He had another option concerning his suspicions about his novel having been published. He could speak out, but he knew only that he might call a representative and hold a discussion about his difficulties.

In University City, near the HEW building, men were going to lunch and had a few smiles for Hoagland, as if to say, "Back so soon? We didn't expect you."

The sun was warmer as spring approached and men sat at red lights eyeing the old brick courtyard of the campus idly.

It seemed that men and women were arriving in swarms. Celebrations and departures were unnoticed by the vile lovers of hate who really meant not to hate, but had ended up with weapons and had not ironed out their psyche. In the fairgrounds atmosphere, people traded secrets freely and then regretted it. The United States was in change, the western coast of Europe was in change. The earth was changing. Moscow was of Philadelphia, Philadelphia of Moscow.

BEFORE YOU LEFT, was a Hoagland poem about, 'heaving casings like a slave with no song.' Hoagland was wandering the apron of the hamburger wrappers swept against the streets the students walked and shopped, dined and played in. It wasn't any later than six in the morning and the bread trucks were servicing the stores along with the milkman and the bakers. The hamburger places were showing signs of opening, but the street was deserted, save for a man dressed in a thin, well-tailored jacket. He was a wide shouldered man and wore fine shoes and put his hands into his coat pockets. Hoagland circled around the intersection, not having had much sleep. He considered going to a suburban town to seek employment at the State Employment office. The man looked up at him and Hoagland looked at the man, noticing his sweater, wondering who he was, thinking that he was in some way familiar. The man looked at Hoagland and said, "Go to your Mama."

Maybe the man was related to Mrs. Leum. Hoagland envisioned what it would be like to depart Philadelphia for Yonkers again, staying with Mrs. Leum. This was before he'd lost the suitcases. He still had the material and it was feasible for him to forget the clouds and tearing of Philadelphia that quiet musing morn in the trembles; and what he saw was a cloudy bird, out of a time period, flying over the spectre of quiet rainy trains, into mid-morning New York, straining to find out what he'd just reorganized, just retasted what he wanted to feel about creation. He saw the later winter hole in the Glamour District (6th Avenue and W. 57th Street) where the people of the streets wore nice scarves and woolen socks and hustled against the wind in an effort to find warm spaces. His last visits to the usually busy New York, had been unusually quiet.

Hoagland left the man. He was excited by the fact that such a respectable looking man would happen to be out by the stands at six in the morning, knowing him well enough to advise him to see Mrs. Leum. Hoagland had packed well the suitcases with manuscripts, recording tapes, songbook, and photographs. In addition, he had pasted carefully a cut out

Philadelphia map upon a looseleaf, readying to do something. He returned to his apartment having had no sleep and sat on his bed, which was a couch. It wasn't even a comfortable couch, just a wooden frame with a thin, flimsy mattress covering it. He thought about his day and thought about seeing Mrs. Leum. He had planned to take a train out to the suburbs of Philadelphia and look into some jobs. He'd also seen trucks going by with Help Wanted signs written on them and one of the places struck his fancy. He started the trek by taking the bus to Center City and made a circle where the office buildings were tall. There were some towers a block and a half west of City Hall. City Hall was the physical center of Philadelphia.

The Delaware area was fifteen blocks to the east and Center City continued fifteen blocks to the west before it ended at the Schuylkill. Hoagland stopped into a lunch place, the sort of place one finds in a metropolis that is for the business crowd. It opened early on the weekday mornings and closed at five or six at night. He had a nervous cup of coffee, feeling pursued again. A man on the street in a suit looked at him and said, "Sorry Hoagland, you've answered too many personals." Hoagland was astonished and pretended he did not know what the man alluded to. Hoagland waved his arms in aggressive defense. Across South Broad Street from the counter place was a huge white police school bus. Hoagland had never seen one like it before and they were suddenly all over town. Hoagland wasn't scared of them, but he thought something very wrong was happening and he hoped it would be solved. No one was in the white buses and he never saw them again. A ruddy looking man inside the coffee shop looked at him dourly. He was a man of grizzled features who had a big, open mouth with large lips and a heavy beard. He was fairly thin and clutched his wallet, looking at Hoagland. Hoagland was muttering under his breath, about going out to Edwardsville.

"Yeah, yeah, go out there," said the slipshod man. "Might be some money in it for you," he said, raising his eyebrows.

Hoagland paid his check, mad for muttering under his breath and raced to the Suburban Philadelphia train station which was very close. He looked at the blackboard with white lettering trying to find the Edwardsville local on the board. His thoughts were being telegraphed into the open air – each well-dressed person seemed a threat to him as he was entering a very paranoid world of his own. The clamor of the station, a bit after midday was exciting to him and the idea of leaving the city very appealing, especially to a part of the area he hadn't seen before. He began to think about the shipyards a counselor had told him about at the end of the Chester local. And he thought about all the things he hadn't done and wished he could afford to do them.

There would be a day when he would, he thought to himself, wondering in the eyes of the people getting aboard the train, whether they knew or cared who he was. He couldn't control his mumblings about the fortunes of the Penn basketball team and what he felt in Philadelphia, but he was trying to rationalize himself.

Next to him he heard some men talking.

"A hotel's been sold in Atlantic City."

"Really?"

"Yes, an old one." Hoagland thought back to the bars in University City. He realized that most of the Atlantic City discussions were taking place on the other side of the Delaware in New Jersey, but it's conversions from an aging resort with a history and a dying future to a vital gambling center had something to do with West Philly. The architecture of the proposed changes was a topic of interest. The investments and the politics also interested the college community.

Some people in Philadelphia were cynical about it, they didn't see how gambling in Atlantic City would change Philadelphia a great deal. It was too far away. It was sixty miles.

"Maybe there'll be more people in the area in general," some suggested, but it was beginning to seem as if Philadelphia would stay as it was, even when gambling commenced in Atlantic City.

Hoagland tried to relax on the train and looked out the window as he passed through small towns which comprised the Philadelphia suburbs. It was a section of greater Philly which had many facets to it. There were industrial concerns in the county, suburban dwellings, and shopping centers, and beyond all of that was wooded land with small inns and large estates. The train terminated at New Hope. Hoagland did not travel that far, finding himself at a junction cut by underpasses and boulevards. The home of the truck with a sign on it turned out to be a small building near a shopping center. Hoagland walked about a half a mile on the shoulder of the road and entered the food distribution plant. "Hello, I saw the sign on your truck. I'm looking for a job."

The bald man looked at Hoagland with an, "are you kidding me?" expression and shrugged. "We got a call from Philadelphia today cancelling the job offer." Hoagland was confused. He'd noticed a fleet of armored cars congregating in West Philly that week. He hadn't seen so many money trucks in all his life. New buildings were shooting up at a record pace.

The sun was generous in Edwardsville and Hoagland walked back toward the train junction. A state police car swerved into a parking lot and looked at him as if to say, "Never make any mistakes, buddy." Hoagland was shaken. He waited at the junction and met a man who worked for the state and he suggested a way Hoagland might get monies from the state. While they waited for the local back to Philadelphia, six spanking new trains roared by them. The man's eyes twinkled and he said to Hoagland, "How do you like them?"

The man told him of a reasonable sum to collect from the state and talked about the new trains. Hoagland thought of the first man by the hamburger stand in West Philly at dawn.

"Nice trains," said Hoagland, "Where are they going?"

"Harrisburg, middle west, all over. There are some yards up here."

Hoagland had discussed the trains very briefly with Broadkey at Le Marin and had noticed a headline in the afternoon paper about the new trains.

He caught the train at the junction and returned into Philadelphia. People eyed him like he was something or someone not really akin to the territory he was riding through. He wasn't. The feeling made him lonely as he viewed the scattered antique barns and shacks still remaining in the suburban sprawl.

Hoagland returned to his apartment and lay down in the sooty sheets. They'd been covered in cigarette ashes since he had given up finding a woman to bring up to his room. His writing mounted in jackets lay side by side in the suitcases. He had a telephone and it was next to his bed on an end table so that he could lie in his bed and set his day up. If there hadn't been so many roaches, he would have had a nice set up. It was functional the way it was, the question was, was Hoagland?

He called Mrs. Leum. Their conversations on the phone were very wild. He took his frustration out on her quite a lot. Many people had taken their frustrations out on Mrs. Leum and she'd grown very bitter about it. There was a time when she could have been accused of being over progressive and experimental, but her spirit had been broken and the anger and dejection blasted at her through phones was something she gave the world back with embittered rhetoric. This time Hoagland was sweet and explained that he was planning to visit her. What he planned to do was try his luck in New York with his writing collection, for New York was the center of the publishing world. He went to the 30th Street Station the next morning and bought a round trip ticket to New York.

It was an old pattern for him by this time to ride to New York from Philadelphia and it took about an hour and forty-five minutes at least to wind through the flatlands in between the two cities and finally cross the Hudson River and enter Pennsylvania Station in midtown Manhattan. The station was in the heart of the Garment District. From there, Hoagland walked, usually lugging bags, past pushcarts, warehouses, through the porno district, over to Grand Central Station, where the Westchester trains left for Yonkers and Euphrates and points beyond.

However, this trip to New York was spent shaking on the train reading the King James Bible from which he felt elevated over the tourists who giggled at him.

He thought of plans. He had to do something immediately. He wanted to do something with his newly organized writing. It oozed of need. His face showed a need to do it, to continue his poem, his swim through rough imagery, and he thought the best and most satisfying way to finance it would be to be paid by somebody for his old material. He called a few companies before leaving Philadelphia and was disappointed that none of them would make an appointment with him. When he arrived in New York, the logical plan was visiting Mrs. Leum and then riding to New York in the morning refreshed to pursue his business. He did not do this. Hoagland walked about the east side of midtown Manhattan, looking at the fancy stores, purchasing an orange and a small cake. He walked into Hunter College. He walked through the Advertising District. He saw women bouncing up and down on their heels.

Finally he entered P.J. Clarke's. It was mid-afternoon. The place was empty. A man with a suit came in, his white hair combed and sat in another corner of the bar. He saw Hoagland's suitcases and advised Hoagland to take the books to Putnam. Hoagland was skeptical.

The man hadn't spoken directly to Hoagland. He'd made the comment indirectly. Hoagland answered indirectly, "Wanna go to Baltimore with me?" Baltimore was a funny place for he and the white haired man to go when they were already in New York, but Hoagland thought the man might enjoy a trip to Baltimore and Johns Hopkins. Hoagland lost his head soon after. He stormed across town, again lugging the bag, hating the bag, forgetting that it contained his 'treasure.'

So he found "The Sad Man" at his office looking weary and under fire in the middle of his work and yelled at "The Sad Man" proclaiming his trip to Washington. He still hadn't concluded that Andrea was just whistling through her teeth the day she pronounced that she and "The Sad Man"might have had his book published. Hoagland never took the white haired man's advice. He had noticed a series of blinking lights on vehicles which seemed to be talking to him during his travels and the lights blinked a definite yellow after his outburst at "The Sad Man".

He rushed downtown, past Penn Station to Greenwich Village. He walked into Nathan's hot dog stand and tough looking men had bullets in their eyes as they watched him. Hoagland realized that he was less safe with them than listening to "The Sad Man." He was frustrated and frightened. He walked back uptown, feet in his heart, his head up his rectum. People poured out of the garment offices and visitors came out of the hotels. He boarded the Philadelphia coach at twilight, holding the cases, and men from Washington sat near him and seemed to be pressuring him about his actions in the past few months. There had been a big drug deal between Euphrates and Philadelphia. Hoagland had befriended a drug pusher around Christmas of 1976 and had told him something he heard a record distributor say. Hoagland was afraid that the two of them had got together and made a big deal. He was scared that he might be arrested for establishing a connection. He reopened the Bible trembling, as the Washington cops tried to lean on his thoughts. They never questioned him directly. His finger followed the words and he tried to hear the patter of young children in the seats ahead of him. It seemed that the train would never arrive in Philadelphia. He'd accomplished nothing in New York, angered "The Sad Man," had not listened to the white haired man, had not called Mrs. Leum, had exhausted his funds and the law had terrified him.

He arrived at his apartment in the cold, grim darkness, shaking and praying. And so it was the next day that he set out for Washington and lost his suitcases. He had called John Barton, hoping he would venture with him to Washington, but John declined, saying, "I might want to come to Philadelphia."

Hoagland said, "Forget it. I'm going to Washington…I've had it.

Ironically, all he could do near Baltimore at the truck stop was call Mrs. Leum and yell at her for losing his suitcases.

"I thought you were coming up here. What are you doing down there?" she said.

This was about time that the willows of love set gratefully into his life. All had been lost, Andrea but a memory, still driving the Westchester route. Dana Broadkey had soured of Hoagland and Hoagland of the life he was leading in the cold University City nights of Le Marin. He wasn't a very good drunk. Igla's illusions had entered, saving Hoagland from suicide and love returned to West Philly in the form of dancing murals, inanity took a vacation replaced by love and schizophrenia went into hiding.

The Cupid aspect of the illusion of Igla was funny. Hoagland thought she was asking him which girl he'd like to marry if everything worked out, and this gave him something to think about. Hoagland had been lost in a wringer of smothered logos and names, but none of the women were real except Andrea and she had told him in the height of their friendship that she had as strong a love for another man. Of course things could change, but Hoagland kept it in mind, for he had thought about solving his problems and returning to Andrea, able to take care of her cheerfully, for what he thought were her real dreams were similar to his. Igla wasn't real to him, illusion or not, but the illusion was a strong feeling he had come to believe in and when it's aura found him, he could believe.

There was a Sunday morning he told himself he would arise and go to the St. Mary's chapel on the Penn campus and find his illusion waiting there and they would have a cup of tea after the service and see if it was an illusion or not. He slept late and never made the service.

Women were the source of mystery in life. That was what had become of his drive. To find out what the thing of life was. He thought of it in a poetic fragment which made no sense. How could anyone say what the thing of life was? He thought, "What were the elements in the vacuum of people's livelihoods in the nectar of knowing how hard it is to discover the valley of wishing wells, light years, it was to discover the valley of time, coming out in the party forever in the seas, there were Queens and this was no myth or legend. Just the healing of God's earth."

He looked at himself, at Philadelphia, as the morning light came through the cracks in his curtains. Earth had to heal, there were cracks in the times of man, but love had to be gained by the multitudes. Hoagland examined his vengeful attitude. If there was hate and the poet had to have a pistol and a bill-fold to secure rights and harbor palaces, to command ships; what was the wishing for lovely ladies worth if their bodies possessed price tags in gathering hotel rooms? He thought of crystal chandeliers. The old people more often than not, slept in separate beds. Their images were of crystal. Hoagland slept in a solitary bed, ready to do something else, despite the mistakes he had made when he traveled blindly and broken.

Mr. Readley and his easel disappeared, a twinkling face as suddenly gone as it had entered. "San Francisco's my kind of town," said Readley to Hoagland before he folded up his easel.

Hoagland felt a debt on the shoulders of some of the characters he was tempted to hate. Everyone would swing through the gates of love. Hadley was on the highway in Westchester grumbling about a class—he had given up some of his adolescent fantasies and was bearing down. He spun on a stool and studied notations on a pad. He had been making many notations. He was plotting points of piano scales like a master geometry professor.

Mr. Broadkey hadn't expected to do anything, but couldn't resist seeing young men get together over something and became the central figure in a musical project about the campus, though his personal problems, just like Hoagland's, were not solved.

Hoagland thought about the wilds of the western region. He hadn't seen anything but population centers, trunk lines, and train schedules. Horses rode through an old western town in his imagination. He saw a ring of high mountains in the background. He saw swinging doors.

In the midst of urbania, it was early at the starting gate when the ponies lined up and the prices were haggled. Suddenly an ominous airplane flew over the sodden street he stood on. Hoagland put the racing program in his pocket. The starting gate at the track was as abstract to him as the Phillies leaving Ohio. They went west. Hoagland remained on the sodden street starving.

What? Igla, Igla, what was she? What about Andrea? "The Sad Man"? Bob Barton. Hoagland sighed, buzz, shhhhh.

In time of tension, Ben Franklin, the flyer of the kite who founded Penn hadn't been around modern spy activity and beside it all, lingual fall out was hanging like tooth decay in the air. Buzz, shhhhhhh, which one?

"You!" said Hoagland to the illusion desperately. He tried to rest his ears from the turmoil. He forgot about the megaphones, the megaphones ceased. In the New York night, the caution lights blinked without Hoagland in town and Igla was on security circuit very strongly changing from the illusion of Igla.

For a second in West Philly, Hoagland Barton and Igla Emmette were the breaker current and the idea was trust and stillness and love. In stillness, maybe all horror ceased, which caused a stir shaking people's souls who craved action. A clinical perception stirred deep within them as they breathed the mocks and stares of nurses. The nurses' confusion was greeted by paychecks and in the fields of life and family. Family had to be preserved in the center. Things moved very quickly in the United States, West Philadelphia version. Hoagland's pain had been amplified and the wounds would be hard to heal.

CHAPTER TWELVE:
WHAT WOULD HOAGLAND DO?

What would Hoagland do? The crown had gone to the sink for a drink and underneath the bridge of his old sorrows was a little fish even though the river was dirtied by years of industries flowing through the electrical north.

The electrical northeast was so hard to deal with and have a glorious time in between working hours. There was always fish to find underneath the stars of golden loves, embroidered by dresses and messes in torment. Like gold, the thoughts were decorative. "The Sad Man" never got off the number.

Hoagland went through the horrors of time drizzly, trying to conceive something inside his graceful heart.   Horror had occurred with him before and he remembered that it needed time to leave. Igla's touch subsided and the winds were in touch with the blowing heads of wheat in distant fields. The horses and cattle smelled fresh and sweet in pastures. The snow on the frosty panes was melting slowly to the days of night when Igla was wishing in the windowsill of sullen relations. It melted sadly for reasons unknown to Hoagland.

ONE

He was in the touristy gallery town of New Hope on the Delaware past Edwardsville, wishing the gas was his, but it wasn't and he bummed a drink from the cute brunette who had given him this ride. The sickly slide of cash into someone elses' pocket washed his tearful eyes, but he liked the way Mr. Readley was thin and wry as he folded up his easel. Hoagland kept some of the serenity Mr. Readley had in his glances.

RIGHT AFTER THE LOSS

Hoagland became a four glance guy momentarily in the HEW office building where he bought papers and cigarettes. The blind counter man was not to be cheated. Hoagland had fights with the bank down below on the ground level at 36th and Market. A check from a job selling tickets for Big Five basketball games was void when it arrived two months late. Hoagland had lost his head so many times in Philadelphia, it was hard to say anything. He blamed some people, and some memories, both fickle and mythful.

When the cowboys came in—they arrived in style with smiling hobos from the desert, but there wasn't a pool hall in University City and food stamps went out daily at the check cashing center.

When something good was happening,

Hoagland could tell by the wave of odd women coming in from different meccas and the gay atmosphere of Philadelphia Greater was mounting so that some had sold out to constant London Broils. Hoagland was thin and hungry. He snatched a box of apple strudels from the door to the hoagie store below his apartment and became his own coffee cup of likeliness.

Missy had come and gone again with the cowboys, while the hoodlums stayed around Hoagland. He was at once talking about pistols, aiming them at himself and at "The Sad Man," trying to direct them away from Igla and others he knew. There had been a few threats and gentlemen who carried guns for a living surfaced in Hoagland's life.

Missy Tillison walked quickly down one of the wrought iron walkways near the old ivy-covered buildings. It looked like she was coming from Le Marin. He was so surprised to see her, he didn't remember that she had blonde hair, but it had been a long time since he'd seen her. No sooner did they have a wink, then she was scurrying the other way in the afternoon of Mr. Readley's easel.

Hoagland had been warned in a theatrical way not to think about intelligence. A man came to his job, dressed in a security guard's uniform, and chatted with him one evening. There were political bosses, underworld czars, and corporate cowboys all slicked together in a computerized shell which amounted to a tangle of roast beef sandwiches. In the midst of a Washington night, near row houses on New York Avenue, a sexy black woman smiles across at Hoagland, "You know "The Sad Man" too?" he asked her. She nods, but it was unclear if they had communicated.

Among the business concerns seeming to be on the edges of the scene in which Hoagland was trying to perceive was oil. He had seen oil in Odessa, Texas from a car window going about fifty-five miles an hour. He'd seen the Union 76 plant in San Pedro and the oil pumps of Signal Hill in Long Beach. He'd heard of the men in the southwest trying to use lignite in the place of petroleum, but so far things like that low grade coal product were only experiments and intelligence people interacted with the oil people. Oil companies financed films and records (now CD's) which were made from vinyl—a byproduct of oil, so Hoagland, being a creative artist, was involved even if he didn't want to be and wouldn't be a complete artist until he figured out oil. He saw the refining plants in Newark and Philadelphia. He saw the petro-chemical plants and marine pipelines of the intercoastal waterways, east and west. He'd seen the vast horizon of the flat Texas desert and Spanish food, not castillian, but Mexican—steaming in plates, while riggings grew in the sky like animals from prehistoric times. He'd not driven anywhere since the oil prices had been raised. The oil concerns, banking concerns, and political and intelligence activities of the United States and abroad were definitely related. And from them stemmed almost any field of interest. He was on an important campus, and originality seemed to set the tempo of the market places he'd seen. The rise and fall of the price and trade values of various currencies was contingent on the demand for goods and business processes used in differing places.

TOO MANY THREADS LIKE WHEAT MADE TO RICE OR PASTA IN THE PROVINCE

Far into the Parisian dusk, the tele'phoniste picked up some complimentary perfume. "Bonne parfum," she said, walking in her sleep under tall trees on the way home to a cozy place. Mrs. Leum had a new compact when she visited Hoagland in West Philly. He'd been eating out of tin cans trying to forget his childhood and his Valentines cards. He'd been smiling then, though someone had told him, to, "Snap out of his daze." Even as a youngster, he had a sleeping quality to him in which he would go out the back door and lose himself to the world of sports. Mrs. Leum looked very unnerved and she fell asleep, depressed by the condition of his apartment.

That's when he found the compact.

The compact said "Made in Paris." Hoagland had had a dream about Rebecca, but his conversation with Broadkey about Rebecca had not made much sense, he only assumed Dana knew of Rebecca, but he never suspected that Mr. Broadkey was familiar with Mrs Leum, but there was certainly a strange atmosphere in West Philly the day she came to town. The fellows at the Vol-Tear Inn seemed to know Mrs. Leum— one said in a voice Hoagland could hear, "Just too good breeding for us." It was as if the man had been in Korea for some time and knew Mrs. Leum from somewhere else.

While Mrs. Leum was sleeping on his crummy bed he looked through some of her things, finding a card with a calendar on it from the community in Long Island of Melville, New York. This made him think of Herman Melville and "Moby Dick" and that put him in a seafaring mood. Hoagland hurriedly checked his map trying to find Melville but couldn't locate it and he sighed thinking of their visit to Le Marin. There was a lad who could be found in Le Marin who was the epitome of the place. French, debonair, and mischievous. The lad dressed in blue naval bell bottoms and a crimped white shirt. He wore a string tie and in the candlelight of the place he walked by Mrs. Leum and Hoagland who were seated at a corner table taking in the characters.

He looked at Hoagland, saying with a smile, "Better watch out for her, she's an informer."

Hoagland cringed, happy to be with Mrs. Leum because she liked to drink coffee in candlelight. She wasn't in the sitting mood at Le Marin and Hoagland was disappointed. He wished that they could have enjoyed the day, but enjoyment was not indicated to Mrs. Leum and after a short beer and a bite at the Vol-Tear, it was back to the apartment where Hoagland revealed the compact and the Melville card. The card reflected in the bell ringing gloom of the campus on a Saturday when everyone is inside because it is inclement.

Hoagland saw the fisheries of the rotaries north of Boston when he looked at the Melville card, like an oar of a fishing vessel in an early legend.

DOUGLAS

Douglas was a Chinese-American man from Flushing, Queens. He had an Uncle in Philadelphia who owned a Chinese restaurant near Race Street in the Chinatown section of Center City.

Hoagland had been speaking with Douglas about certain things as they contemplated a project or two. Dana had introduced them in Le Marin. Douglas was a junior at Penn. Dana had hoped they might collaborate on something and Hoagland was enchanted by the rivers of fine tobaccos which flowed from Douglas' room in an old fraternity hall of the campus which was certainly a prime place to live.

Snow was on the ground near Le Marin and tinsel in the pines near Christmas time, the day Hoagland found the sheet music for the French duets in a music store in Center City. He brought the book to Dana who spun it over to Doug and Doug recorded an album. One very impressive thing about Douglas was that he built and repaired pianos, actually working with the rods inside the wood.

GERALD

This was about the time a young black man was holed up in a hamburger stand in the cold airs of December sipping coffee. Hoagland was a bit high and found himself chattering with the fellow who said he had just been thrown out of his girlfriend's apartment in North Philly and so Hoagland invited him to stay in the dingy flat and they awoke, on a Sunday, Hoagland not knowing for sure who the visitor was.

Gerald said he was from Natchez, Mississippi and that he spoke French. He listed his occupation as painter, but didn't have any portfolio with him. He seemed interested in Montreal, and Hoagland showed him an application to gain working papers in Switzerland. Hoagland also noted that Gerald pointed out to Hoagland that Pearl Street in Baltimore might be cosmic for Hoagland in some way.

In the most recent past, Gerald had been busy dodging the Philadelphia Police Department while camping out amongst the concrete canyons of Market Street and South Broad Street.

Hoagland and Gerald ended up in Doug's room smoking Export A tobacco and looking at the pianos in the living room as the Fraternity House brothers prepared for a meal. Gerald depressed a key of one of the pianos like he might have a natural gift for music as well. The white man, black man, and China-man looked like an advertisement for American Civil Rights. Doug assured his frat brothers that the socializing with street people would be alright. The spirit of the friendship with Gerald lasted years after they knew each other in West Philly. They had talked late into the nights at Hoagland's apartment. Hoagland was still hoping to see Andrea, and wondering in the explosion of the meaning of his visitor at work, who had shook him, along with the lost paycheck so much that he failed to report to the security job again and was suddenly in a shambles with friends instead of being depressed with a job. This was before the willows of love set in, but Doug and Gerald were a part of the willows of love.

Mrs. Leum had something on her mind the day she came. By that time, Gerald had passed through Hoagland's life. Doug had seen that Hoagland was distressed and finished the music project on his own, hoping that Hoagland would wake up his lithographic mind and excel. It had been something of seeing a design and the core of finery and object value and sensory taste for Hoagland to mix with Doug and Broadkey. The experience was in his eyes, if his clothes and acts didn't show it at the moment. Mrs. Leum had something on her mind, but Hoagland couldn't tell what it was. He was perplexed and this began his sessions of staring deep into her tired eyes to try and unlock the story never told to him about himself, she and "The Sad Man." The campus bells tolled as Mrs. Leum slept on the couch, but Hoagland couldn't piece together Mrs. Leum's secret connections with various cities. It was true that he'd been getting anonymous phone calls as had Doug, and they were worried about this.

Hoagland kept Doug in touch with his previous mistakes, cautioning Doug where he might go wrong. He thought he saw Doug's soul in his printed dream and that the hard rock music was a form Doug might get talked into if Doug didn't realize that his talent surpassed most of the famous rock and roll stars.

The activity in Yonkers was never very sure, for being a bordering community of New York, Yonkers was overlooked oft times, creating an opportunity for the amply-sized town to be full of many mysteries. Mrs. Leum was terrorized in Yonkers by her own futility and by the way Yonkers was. It was a rough town with snapping dogs. It had big factories along the Hudson with towers filled with syrups and chemicals, and rail lines going under bridges. Mrs. Leum, Louette Leum, was alone and scared. Her biggest fear was for Hoagland, she was a dedicated mother.

DOG FOOD

"Dog food," the box said. John Barton had brought him things in a dog food box. Hoagland sometimes took things like this far too seriously. Mrs. Leum's face was finally caving in after twenty five years, seven or eight in complete conflict with "The Sad Man," yet never telling Hoagland the whole story. Hoagland guessed that some of her story was not true. She could tell stories about her California family for hours on end, but Hoagland wondered whether his mother really hailed from France or Long Island; Philadelphia or Brooklyn. He thought she knew people in Philadelphia society, like the lad in the bell bottoms at Le Marin.

Hoagland thought about the Hudson River.

Mrs. Leum left his apartment and drove back to Yonkers. Eugene Ormandy, in his twilight, still conducted the Philadelphia Orchestra. The orchestra had maintained it's matchless reputation through the years and Hoagland had dug the depth of Mrs. Leum's record collection trying to make an association with her and Philadelphia. He remembered that there was a time that the family had driven down an avenue of cobblestone (probably Rising Sun Avenue) in a driving rain storm waiting for "The Sad Man" to depart an engagement. This was in the late fifties. Were any of "The Sad Man's" associates at the State of Pennsylvania Bicentennial Commission conference in 1975 also at the Rising Sun engagement in 1959? The people in Le Marin seemed to know Mrs. Leum and Hoagland identified the fine French bar and restaurant with the family's days in Washington when Mrs. Leum had thrown dinner parties on their Northwest terrace during glorious June weather. Mrs. Leum had stopped playing the piano before Hoagland was born

and she might have lost most of her Hot Club
of France associates, this vaguely crept into
her mind as she drove over the chimneys of
North Philadelphia where Gerald had been
living, through the woods of the Dutch, the
forests of the Germans, to the pipelines and
tankers of the Jersey flats.

She paused in her usual style for a long
cup of coffee alone at a rest area. She cried
near Fort Lee, that bottomless burgh which
hung on the cliffs by the George Washington
Bridge. She laughed giddily as she wound
around the aging concrete turn-about which
led to the West Side Drive leading north
under tree cover and blazing winter's river
sunset. She passed by the high rises of
Riverdale, laughed and cried as she hit the
Yonkers border, thinking of her father limp-
ing up a South Yonkers staircase to make a
hardware sale right before he died. She
drove past John Barton's and thought about
placing a call to her friend in northern
Westchester, but her friend was doing well
and Mrs. Leum didn't want to bother her.

Hoagland hungrily ate the bread she had brought him, as the sun departed for another cool evening and he wondered if Gerald would visit in the dead of night as he was accustomed to. Hoagland enjoyed this most of the time being a night person, but wondered about Gerald and decided to see if anyone in the soul club on South Street knew Gerry, for he did not want to harbor a fugitive. Gerald was known to be a wanderer they said, he'd been up and down in Baltimore, in the off beat neighborhoods of New York, in the ghetto of Boston, around the coastal ways, never by sea, but thinking of traveling by sea from Canada north and east to England.

LOCAL BADMEN

With the onset of the local badmen sent to disuade Hoagland from talking about the drug deal, Hoagland began to turn to Andrea in his despair and tried to figure out what was known about the film bosses at the bar near the Delaware.

Kerry had done her undergraduate work at Georgia Tech and along with Paco were graduates of Penn's Wharton School of Business. Andrea's work in Buffalo had been good enough to get her in the Newmarket Company. The three of them hung out together during the bicentennial occasionally, they were around the same age and enjoying a fast social life.

When Hoagland had originally returned from New York after juggling with Milt, and the line of DMT where he perceived what the police megaphones told him to forget, the four of them had gone to Le Marin for a drink. Paco and Kerry were delighted for some reason to see Hoagland's heart broken over Andrea.

A few days later, Hoagland was on the haldols and forced a friendly dance with the same three in a place in West Philly called Smokey Joe's—a sort of dug out place where food was sold. The lights were low and the prices were not high. Paco, originally from Louisville, talked about his days at Wharton when he was a regular at Smokey Joe's.

It got to the point of the year when the men on the T.V. screens of the bars were blocking and tackling in football poses. The Phillies had just failed against the Reds in the National League playoffs, but it had been quite a year for them.

Hoagland was having a beer alone at Smokey Joe's later, say the beginning of November '76, thinking about Paco's career at Wharton. He had noticed that there were a few publications at Penn, including a business magazine published by Wharton. He now made a link between the guy with the portable T.V. at security who seemed like a Warner Brothers G.I. and the current edition of the Wharton Magazine which featured a picture of Humphrey Bogart and a tough looking blonde dish. Hoagland realized that central casting was trying to move him over to the side of the road in the midst of the old talkies. Hoagland decided to be flattered.

Hoagland had written a nutty song called "The Queen of Prussia" about a public relations stunt Newmarket had run to stimulate business one Sunday where Andrea had dressed up as the two of spades and Kerry was costumed as the Queen of Hearts. Kerry had grown up in suburban King of Prussia, Pennsylvania. Hoagland had suggested a wine tasting room for Front Street, and when one was opened he became incensed, thinking the Wharton crowd had capitalized while he was on public assistance and stelazine.

BOSTON OR BUST

The willows of love had set in alright and it was on a late winter's day that Hoagland left Philadelphia for what would be the last time. John Barton had come down to pick him up and Hoagland gave the keys to the manager down in the hoagie shop. They drove northwest through Fairmount Park, past Mount Airy, into Chestnut Hill. They turned there for the expressway which would take them back to New York. They stopped for something to eat near Chestnut Hill. Two guys with charcoal grey suits on greeted them. The conversation was light on the way back to New York. Hoagland felt some kind of relief at getting out of Philadelphia. He spoke of wanting to go to the country, Columbia County (N.Y.) maybe.

They arrived at John Barton's apartment in a couple of hours. His wife was there sipping a soda. She greeted Hoagland and Hoagland had a rough night hearing voices from down below the apartment building saying they were from Philadelphia International Records. He thought he heard Gerald's voice and was tempted to run outside and start cheering, "Gerr-ee, jerr-i!"

The streets of South Yonkers were all soft and aglow next morning, the birds sang from the trees. Hoagland went to the laundromat on Broadway with John Barton and while they were there, Hoagland hauled off and struck John Barton to which it seemed a parade of Cadillacs passing by, applauded. By nightfall Hoagland was hot on the idea of going to Columbia County and John Barton lent him the money to go to Albany by train and a little extra to get to Columbia County from Albany.

He got on the train at the Yonkers station and rode the local train to Croton where he changed for the Albany train. There was kind of an excitement on the train and Hoagland scribed furiously his new novel, anxious to replace what was lost in the suit-cases. He got to Albany and was at the train station when he heard a voice say, "We might not want to see you in Albany, but you might want to go back to Boston." Hoagland was sold. He took a taxi downtown where the bus station was. He bought a ticket to Boston. The bus rattled it's way across western Massachusetts into Boston. It pulled into the Greyhound Station, near the Boston Hilton at about six in the morning.

He walked near Haymarket Square. He stopped into a restaurant and had some tea. There were a host of redheaded ladies in the restaurant. He thought he saw Igla's mother, but he had never met her before.

Igla was a redhead and so was Hoagland.

One of their plans in their only meeting was to start an organization for redheads. Boston was full of redheads. Hoagland hoped he'd see Igla, but knew the chances were slim. She wasn't in the telephone directory anymore. She came from the suburbs, southwest of Cambridge. Also he had to fight the feeling that every redhead or chiffon blonde he saw, looked like Igla. Igla, Igla, he had her on his mind. He traced every freckle, every cell of the female redheaded anatomy.

The next place he went was on a small alley down the street from the restaurant. It was a bar where early Sunday morning horse racing fans hung out. A Philadelphia horse man also owned the Philadelphia 76'ers basketball team. Hoagland wondered if he was into action literature. He had this man on his mind when he entered the bar. A racing program from Garden State Race Track, near Philadelphia, had been thrown on the street outside Hoagland's West Philly apartment. One horse entered in that program was, "Freeze Out." Hoagland had long ago seen a Paul

Newman movie called, "The Hustler," which used the term freeze out in relation to pool.

"A hundred dollar freeze out, winner take all," is uttered by Newman in this movie. In the world of lone wolves and hustlers, the words, 'freeze out,' became a warning that one was losing his cool. Paul Newman had his thumbs broken after winning the game of eight ball.

So Hoagland watched himself in the horse racing bar as the shots began to pour and he checked his curiosity about the Philadelphia sportsman. There were a few gnatty, likely customers in the bar, but nothing really developed. Hoagland did tell one man, he looked like a good guy, about his lost suitcases. The man offered his condolences.

Next Hoagland went over to Haymarket Square and watched the people prepare for the weekly crafts exhibition. He wrote in his pad as pretty girls with ribbons in their hair passed by. "Is that Igla?" Wait a minute. He stood near an elevated highway and a young black boy came by and said hello.

Hoagland took the streetcar all the way to

Newton and ran around the Boston College buildings for a second. There was a certain magic in the air. Hoagland felt drawn toward societies. From Boston, from Philadelphia, from New York, from Memphis, these women and their parents drew close to Hoagland and he felt pins in his fingers as he reboarded the streetcar with his pad and headed back downtown.

He entered the Bradford Hotel and found a room to write in. From a church tower he heard bells ringing. He wrote about a printer from Bowdoin. This was a dream. A young writer meets a printer and from there a book is published.

He headed out toward Brookline on the Cleveland Circle car. He stopped in a Chinese restaurant. It was getting late in the March day. He called up Jim Wentworth in a town called North Reading. Jim said he would pick up Hoagland at the end of the Green Line at the Lechemere Station. Hoagland hustled back to the red car and took it to Park Street. He changed for the Green

Line and Jim Wentworth, waiting with nifty compact car, picked him up at Lechemere.

Jim was a good guy, an old friend from Euphrates High School. He was another who had gone to college in Boston and stayed. He was working for Tufts University as a computer researcher. He actually programmed himself and did research work on the keyboard. The ride out to North Reading was accomplished on a nice, new highway. They passed Salem Street and Hoagland was reminded of Arthur Miller's, "The Crucible," and stories of the Salem witch trials.

They talked about things old friends talk about. People from Euphrates, things on their minds. At one point Hoagland thought he heard Jim say that Igla was in the apartment upstairs, but he didn't know that Jim knew Igla. They had something to eat and talked into the night. Hoagland put a record on and fell asleep.

The next morning they woke up bright and early. Jim had to go to work down in Medford. In the kitchen, while drinking coffee,

Hoagland got into a discussion on printing and computers with Jim. He offered Jim a chance to start a partnership with Hoagland, but Jim wasn't interested. Jim did shed some light on computers and printing. They rode down to Medford. When they got to Tufts, Jim gave Hoagland twenty dollars to get back to New York.

Hoagland boarded a bus and then grabbed a cab to Arlington, on Massachusetts Avenue where he had spotted a printer in the phone book. But there was no print shop at the address Hoagland had given the taxi driver and Hoagland was out fifteen dollars. He noticed on Mass. Ave. a whole string of stores made to order for him. There was the Three Acres, Paul's Gift Shop, Rentals Stables Appliances, and Marie's Wedding Gowns. Marie was one of Andrea's nicknames. Hoagland thought someone from Le Marin had planted the store after reading his poem, "Marie from Montreal." Hoagland went into a frenzy thereafter and returned to Copley Square. He wrote in the Public Library for a time.

The symbolism of "Copley Square" as in 'coppin dope' was a bad place for the library to be, a bad place for anything to be.

Being poor is hard, but a trick with a woman or man will only cause worse problems. By the same token, people with money have a responsibility not to offer money for sex, or go along with an offer.

"There must be an honest woman out there somewhere!" Hoagland prayed.

He was in Back Bay late at night. He decided to go to the Riverside station of the M.T.A. He boarded a subway for Wellesley. He rode the canal like ride through the quiet woods of established settlements near Boston. The man at the horse racing bar had gotten in touch with the Philadelphia sportsman. He told him of Hoagland's suitcases. Hoagland got to Riverside station near Wayland. The greyhound bus to New York also stopped there. He got off the subway and walked through the bus area back out onto the subway platform. There was a drive-

way there.   Suddenly a grey Valiant with
Louisiana plates pulled into the driveway.
Hoagland couldn't believe it. It was the man
with the suitcases. He had been contacted by
C.B. He decided to drive up to Boston from
Delaware and return the cases. He had a
smile on his face as he opened the car door.
Hoagland met the man at the car door and out
came the two suitcases; one was blue denim,
the other, leather. Hoagland thanked the man
who shrugged off a cup of coffee, he had to
be back on the road again.

Hoagland seized his suitcases and boarded
the subway for downtown Boston again. The
night was almost out. He returned to the
Back Bay section of town, hanging out in the
railroad station for a few hours until sun-up.

When business started up again, Hoagland
headed into town and found a printer on Milk
Street. Hoagland showed him a copy of "The
Early Voyages" asking him if he wanted to
print it. The printer said no, but that Hoagland ought to try a place on Congress Street.

John's Printing on Congress Street was

what Hoagland had been hoping to find. John was an older man with a white face and two patches of grey hair on each side of his bald head. Hoagland showed him the manuscript to "The Early Voyages" and John scrutinized it very closely before looking up and saying, "I like it."

He offered a deal where by John would print the book on a loan, paid back by Hoagland from the book sales. They started work on the printing job right away. Hoagland did the final proofreading in John's office. When the proofreading was finished, Hoagland left the magic of John's office. His life had now become a success. He had always wanted to publish a book. He hurried back to Back Bay Station, his heart in a whirl. It was time to tell Mrs. Leum. He called her collect in Yonkers and she was bubbling. She had always wanted her son to publish a book. "Mom, I'm getting my book published! The man returned the suitcases and a printer in Boston has agreed to take it on!" he exclaimed.

"That's wonderful dear," she said.

John had said he would have two thousand copies in about two weeks. John had also agreed to help with the promotion of the book which included a party, and Hoagland decided to have the party in Euphrates on Warburton Avenue in a little bookstore next to a bar he had often gone to.